BOOK OF THE BLOODLESS VOLUME ONE

ALTERNATIVE AFTERLIVES

BOOK OF THE BLOODLESS
VOLUME ONE

ALTERNATIVE AFTERLIVES

CHRISTOPHER FIELDEN

Victorina Press
www.victorinapress.com

Book of the Bloodless Volume 1: Alternative Afterlives

Copyright © 2019 Christopher Fielden
www.christopherfielden.com

First published 2019 by Victorina Press
Adderley Lodge Farm
Adderley Road
Market Drayton, TF9 3ST
England

First Edition

British Library Cataloguing in Publication Data
A catalogue record for this book is available from the British
library.

Cover and interior artwork © 2019 David Whitlam
Interior design and layout: Christopher Fielden

ISBN: 978-1-9993696-6-8

Printed in Great Britain by 4edge Limited

DEDICATION

For all those people who want to believe in something,
but aren't sure what that something is.

CONTENTS

INTRODUCTION

One of my most vivid memories from childhood concerns death. I was about 10 or 11 years old and I was having a bath. I remember thinking about what would happen when my life was over. At that age it was hard to comprehend, so I decided to concentrate on one simple thought:

When I die, I will be gone forever.

I thought about this carefully, allowing the concept to sink in.

The infinite past didn't bother me – it occurred before I existed – but the eternal future made me feel uneasy. I realised that I'm not immortal and, when my life ends, eternity will continue without me. I felt numb. My vision clouded. I saw black. I remember lurching up in the bath, feeling scared and disoriented.

After that experience, I avoided thinking about death. Over time, my ruminations became less significant, although never forgotten.

Later in life, as I worked on my writing, I found most of my stories involved death or the afterlife. Some are about zombies or undead creatures. Others concern characters dying and passing on to another place.

Sometimes I start stories with no intention of death being involved. Then a demonic or angelic character will come along, or my protagonist will be transported to a realm beyond life. Do I have a subconscious obsession with the topic, haunted by my experience in the bath? Maybe. Whatever the reason, it's a strong theme that everyone can relate to; we all die.

The idea of an existence after death is comforting. However, the idea of an all-powerful entity (or entities) doesn't seem plausible to me. While I respect the opinions of those who believe in gods and religious texts, I've found I can't share their suspension of disbelief; I can't believe in something that's intangible.

We understand little about our existence, the planet we live on, the solar system it resides in and the universe. There's no way of knowing what lies beyond life. It could be nothing. It could also be anything.

The logical part of me is an atheist. Science doesn't support the idea of an afterlife, or that gods exist. However, the little boy in the bath is an agnostic. He wants there to be something. Needs there to be something.

That belief – that there *could* be *something* – is what I explore in many of my stories. Some are positive. Some are of nightmares. Most lie somewhere in-between.

I hope you enjoy reading the stories in this book as much as I have enjoyed writing them.

Chris Fielden, February 2019

~

ALTERNATIVE AFTERLIVES

DEATH OF A SUPERHERO

'Name?'

'Batman.'

Death looked up from where he was seated on the Throne of Bones, behind the Desk of Deliverance, in front of Death's Door. Although dressed like Batman, the person standing before him didn't exhibit the level of physical fitness you might expect from a successful crime fighting vigilante. There was an unacceptable similarity between their height and girth. Said similarity would probably make leaping from buildings, running quickly or fitting into the Batmobile somewhat problematic. The person also seemed to possess a general lack of understanding regarding Batman's gender.

'Nice suit,' said Death.

'Thanks.'

Batman obviously had no concept of sarcasm either.

Death looked back at his Recent Expirees' Manifest. He tapped the page with a bony finger.

'You're listed here as Doris Claymore,' he said.

'Never heard of her,' said Batman.

Death reached out and stroked the decaying blade of the scythe that rested against his desk. 'This is quite simple, Doris. To progress peacefully into the afterlife, you need to confirm your name. It means I can be certain of who you are, what you've achieved in life and, therefore, where you should spend eternity.' Death dished out his best glare. As glares go, it was pretty impressive. In the past, it'd made stars think twice about shooting. 'Will you tell me your real name, please?'

'Already told you. I'm Batman.'

'How can I put this politely?'

'No need to be polite,' said Bat-Doris. 'Got skin as thick as armadillos, us crime fighters.'

Given the invitation, Death decided to be blunt. 'Not only is Batman fictional, *he*...' Death left a pause, which he hoped would scream with meaning, '...is a man.'

'And?'

'You have breasts.'

'They're pecs.'

'No, they're breasts,' said Death, 'and Lycra does little to mask their magnitude. I feel I should add that Batman was always depicted as an athletic individual, at the peak of physical fitness. Clearly, you're not.'

A tear trickled from beneath Doris's mask, suggesting her skin might not be as thick as she'd led Death to believe. 'OK,' she whispered, 'point taken.'

Despite the scythe, the rotting cloak and the distinct lack of flesh coating his crumbling bones, Death was a sensitive individual. He disliked causing upset. Most people found the experience of dying traumatic enough, without him being disagreeable.

In a gentler tone, he said, 'Good. What's your real name?'

'Bruce Wayne.'

Death took a moment. His was the greatest of jobs, an eternal vocation no other would ever undertake. The pride he felt in this most trusted position was indescribable, the honour overwhelming. Still, on certain days the downsides of immortality became glaringly apparent and he realised how lucky mortals were to die. This was one of them.

'You're not Bruce Wayne,' said Death, deciding it was time to unleash some even harder truths. 'Or Batman. Your name is Doris Claymore and in life you were a decidedly non-superhuman nurse.'

Another tear appeared beneath the mask and trickled down Doris's chubby cheek. Death felt guilty. He'd allowed irritation to control his words, creating insults when he should be showing more respect. Eternal life would be dull without the challenges people like Doris presented.

One of the lessons he'd learned by existing for as long as things had been dying was the art of patience. It would be a shame to forget that lesson today. There would be a reason why Doris was behaving in this manner. It was Death's duty to discover the reason and deal with it. He decided to try a different tack.

'How did you die, Doris?'

'I was doing some vigilante stuff. You know, chasing a psycho across rooftops, that kind of thing.'

'And?'

'I did a jump from one building to another. And missed.'

Given that Doris probably had a bodily mass similar to that of an adolescent rhino, it wasn't hard to imagine gravity prevailing while she battled with thrust, momentum, distance and the laws of physics.

'That's exactly what I have written here,' said Death.

'See, I'm telling the truth.'

'Next to the name Doris Claymore.'

'Must be a typo.'

'It also says that you were at a superhero convention, had a Jägerbomb or 17...' Death paused and double-checked the number, '...a Jägerbomb or 17 too many and got a bit carried away. Does that sound familiar, Doris?'

'Stop calling me Doris.'

A tremble in Doris's voice caused Death to look carefully at the woman standing before him. Fear danced in her eyes and she kept glancing over his shoulder.

'It's the door, isn't it?' asked Death.

Doris nodded.

Death's Door was huge and set into a wall of light behind the Desk of Deliverance. The portal was sinister, black and fleshy. Blood oozed from its surface, which gave the impression the door might be alive, but only just. Death often wished he could alter its appearance, and the foul smell that emanated from it, but there were always barriers to major changes in the Realm Beyond Life, including politics, beings who believed they were gods, the dead's expectations and laws dictating The Way Things Should Be. Sometimes it was easier not to bother.

'It's going to judge me, send me to Hell,' said Doris.

'Judgement is my job,' Death replied, 'and there's no such place as Hell.'

'You said what I've done in life tells you where I should spend eternity.'

'I did.'

'I haven't done anything.' Doris looked at the door again. 'Well, I've done plenty, but none of it was much use.'

'And Batman did lots of good things, right?'

Doris nodded. 'I'm going to a bad place, aren't I?'

Death looked back at his notes. 'You were a nurse in a children's hospital. It says here that you were good with children. You could put them at ease, even in the most difficult of circumstances.'

'Anyone can do that.'

Death shook his skull. 'It's a difficult thing to do. I can see why you sought escapism by drinking and playing superheroes. But you were gifted. You did a great deal of good with your life. You helped others.'

'Lots of people help others.'

'True. But you... You were better at it than Batman.'

A smile crept onto Doris's lips. 'You're good at this.'

'Thank you,' said Death.

Doris pulled off her mask. 'Sorry if I was difficult.'

Death saw that all the tension had left her. She looked radiant and, more importantly, ready to state her title.

'What is your name?' asked Death.

'Doris Claymore.'

Death stood, hefted the scythe and tapped it against the door. There was an unpleasant squishing sound. Fresh blood oozed from the door's surface. As if this meant some toll had been paid, the portal swung open, revealing Doris's pathway: a glimmering road that led through stars and galaxies towards the Ever.

'This is your path beyond life, Doris Claymore,' said Death. He reached out and touched Doris's forehead with a bony finger. A small glowing mark appeared on her skin. 'May it bring you peace.'

Doris stepped through the doorway and embraced eternity. The door shut behind her. Death rested his scythe against the desk and sat on his throne.

'Next,' he said, looking through the manifest, trying to find his place.

He heard some shuffling footsteps.

Without looking up, he said, 'Name?'

'Wonder Woman,' replied a gruff voice.

'For fuck's sake,' said Death.

~

ALTERNATIVE AFTERLIVES

DEVIL'S CRUSH

1

The problem with inhabiting a body with legs for 35 years is that I became accustomed to having legs. When those limbs were taken from me, I thought my subconscious would catch up quickly and I'd instinctively regard myself as legless. I was wrong.

It's been almost two years since my date with the grenade. Yet still I wake up oblivious to the fact that I'm missing limbs. Moments ago I swung myself out of bed, thinking to walk to the kitchen for a drink. I embraced the morning, and the floor, with a thud. I swore, I cursed, I laughed. What else could I do? If I were unable to laugh at the ridiculous broken mess I've become, I think I'd deteriorate like Steve. At war he lost an arm, a foot and half his face. Back home he lost his mind. Watching him deteriorate into a lifeless husk was hard. Could I watch my own body wither along with my personality? No. The same will not happen to me.

I struggle into my wheelchair, making a mental note to invest in some 25 millimetre tufted-twist-pile carpet to make my morning routine less painful, and trundle into the kitchen.

The first thing that strikes me is the stink of fire. I can see no smoke, no blackened furniture, no indication of a blaze. Aside from the smell, the kitchen is exactly as I left it, apart from one small detail. There's a bottle in the middle of the kitchen table.

I edge my chair forward to look more closely. The bottle is filled with red liquid that dances like fire. On the front is a label that reads, 'Devil's Crush'.

Intrigued, I pick the bottle up and almost drop it; I wasn't expecting it to be hot. I sniff the bottle, trying to determine if it's the source of the burning smell. It isn't. I turn the bottle over. On the back is another label. Underneath some text that is too small to read, it says, 'Made in Hull'. Somehow, this seems apt.

As I study the strange liquid, wondering if the 'u' in Hull might be a misprint, I hear someone clear their throat behind me. Instantly, I drop the bottle into my lap and swing my chair around. The 9mm Browning L9A1 I keep tucked beneath my chair's cushion is in my hand without me having to think.

As I take in my surroundings I realise the bottle had captivated my attention so fully that I'd forgotten my training. Questions fill my mind. Why didn't I clear the room? Why had the bottle intrigued me so? And how could I have failed to notice the demon in the corner?

There are black hoof-prints scorched into the kitchen's tiled floor. He's sitting on a chair that appears to be made of iron. It glows beneath his bulk.

I know the demon is a he because he's naked. He's a he with the right to be proud of just how much of a 'he' he is. His skin is the colour of burnt rust, his body slender, yet muscular, and he wears a goatee on his chin more like the animal it is named after than a man. His two horns are long and curved like warped blades of molten rock, his hairline a mass of flickering flames and in his eye sockets are two glowing coals, which ping and hiss like the embers of a dying fire. He is the source of the acrid stench that fills the room.

'I'm sorry to interrupt at such an ungodly hour,' he says in an unnaturally deep voice. 'Put the gun away. It is useless to you.'

I do as he commands, not because I want to, but because I am unable to disobey. There's a mesmerising quality to his voice, which I realise I will have to fight if I want to act of my own free will.

'Are you Sergeant Joshua Purvis?' he asks.

I'm aware that I'm gawping. I try to say, 'Yes,' but all that escapes from my mouth is a slurping mumble. I decide to forget talking and nod.

'Do you know who I am?'

'Satan?' I guess, pleased that I manage to speak.

He snorts laughter, smoke spiralling from the holes in his face that I assume must be nostrils. 'No,' he says. 'My name is Colin.'

I hear myself snigger.

'I've taken a human name to seem less threatening,' Colin continues, in a tone that suggests he is only imparting this information so he won't find it necessary to tear my head off. 'Names aside, you must concur, my master has excelled with the physical manifestation conjured for my eternal servitude.'

I find myself unable to disagree.

Colin rises slowly from his chair and takes a step towards me. His horns score black marks into the ceiling.

'I'm dreaming,' I state, rather than asking a question to which I may not like the answer.

'No,' says Colin. I can feel my scepticism manifesting itself as a squint about my eyes. Seeing this, Colin moves forward and pinches my arm. I scream in pain, not just from the pinch of the serrated talons that are Colin's fingertips, but at the impossible heat, which emits from his body.

He takes a step backwards, politely waiting for me to stop swearing, then says, 'Point taken?'

I nod. At least the pain has helped me to focus. I can think and speak again. 'Why are you here?'

'To deliver the Devil's Crush.'

'To me?'

'Yes. It's a gift.'

'From?'

'My master.'

'Why is your master sending me gifts?'

'You possess a skill we wish to employ.'

'So this isn't a gift?'

Colin smiles, as if pleased with me, revealing a myriad of teeth like needles. 'It depends on which way you look at it.'

I pick the bottle back up and watch the fiery liquid writhe within. 'Am I supposed to drink it?' I ask.

'I believe so.'

'What happens if I don't?'

'Nothing.'

'What happens if I do?'

'Your legs will grow back.'

Now he has my interest. 'And what must I give in return?'

Colin subjects me, quite literally, to a burning stare. 'Oh, you know,' he says, 'the usual stuff about the sale of your soul. It's all in the small print on the back of the bottle.'

Immediately my instincts tell me to say no. I've never heard a story where the selling of one's soul ends well. But I feel a tingle of hope and I don't want it to stop. I've been to Afghanistan. I came back crippled. Living in this body is a lonely misery beyond imagining. I have no doubt there is trickery behind Colin's offer, but could it be worse than the life I currently endure? I could have my legs back. To me, that sounds more appealing than a sauna full of voluptuous nymphomaniacs. At least with legs I could enter said sauna without fear of humiliation. At the moment, I can barely summon the courage to leave my home. Day by day, although I fight it, I increasingly understand the mental spiral that led Steve to take his own life.

'I must press you for an answer,' says Colin.

'Deal,' I say. Before Colin can say anything else I uncork the bottle and swallow the liquid. It burns, sweet mercy, it burns so badly. I fall from my chair, coughing, gagging. I clutch at my throat and try to scream before my consciousness goes AWOL.

2

My head throbs and my mouth is dry. I'm in the kitchen, on the floor, my chair tipped over on its side. I rub my eyes and look around. The stink of fire is absent from the air. There is no bottle, no scorched footprints on the floor, no Colin.

A mirthless chuckle escapes my lips. These new anti-depressants have some weird hallucinogenic side-effects. I struggle to my feet and walk to the bathroom. It isn't until I'm dropping my boxers that I realise I have legs. Not just any legs, they're my legs, right down to the scar on my right shin and the two freckles on my left kneecap.

I look at myself in the mirror and giggle. The elation rising in me is frightening. It's not that I'm scared of the joy this moment holds. It just feels weird, realising how long it's been since I've felt any happiness.

Pulling up my boxers, I run into the kitchen and smell the stench of burning.

'Hello, Joshua,' says Colin. He is as he was before: Tall, hot and demonic.

'Shit.'

He shrugs. 'Should have read the small print.'

Then Colin rips my head off.

3

I have legs and my head is back where it should be. I'm on top of a colossal tower. It's the tallest edifice in the endless cityscape before me by some order of magnitude. The city is a sprawling mass of twisted buildings, all incredible and hewn from rock the colour of the moon. They look like they've been designed by an architect with a narcotic dependency.

'Where are we?'

'Helven,' Colin replies. He's standing next to me, smouldering.

'Oh, I get it, a cross between Heaven and Hell.'

Colin shakes his head. 'There are no such places. There is only Helven, the city of angels and demons.'

The mention of angels brings back unwanted memories, for I've witnessed them dying. It's how I lost my legs. One second my platoon was shooting at people who were shooting at us. The next second, a mother and child ran into the line of fire and we were shooting at them. Somehow they made it into the middle of the street without being hit and huddled, confused and scared, dressed in rags. Then I caught sight of a grenade in the downward arc of a lob. I ran forward. I still have no idea what I hoped to achieve; they were too far away. I saw smeared tears on the child's cheeks. *Bang*. They were consumed by the explosion and I parted company with my legs.

'How else do you think we maintain balance?' Colin continues. 'Nature doesn't just rule on Earth. She rules here too. If there were places where only good or evil existed, well, it just wouldn't work, would it?' He talks so bluntly, I find myself believing him. His voice still carries that hypnotic edge.

Hypnosis aside, I've never been a big believer in Heaven and Hell. If I'm honest, I didn't know what to believe. All I can say with certainty is that whatever I expected, this wasn't it. Helven is magnificent, but Colin seems to belong here, which gives the place an alien quality I find unsettling.

'So, what happens now?'

'There's a debate in progress at which your presence is required. The voice of Fire is arguing about cacodemons' rights with the leader of the opposition. They are very badly treated here, particularly by an extreme right-wing group of sprites.'

'Cacodemons?'

'Yes.' I nod like I understand, which prompts Colin to motor on. 'Then there is some argument to be had about volcanic eruptions on Earth – the Fire party feel there are too many humans now and a catastrophe would help restore balance, whereas the Light party believe humanity should have another chance to redress the problem themselves. Then there's the manifesto of the murdered, decreeing the laws of vengeance—'

'Sorry to interrupt, but my head hurts,' I say. 'What do I have to do?'

Colin moves over to an opening in the vast roof space. 'Follow me.'

Moving towards him, I see fairy-tale stairs spiralling

downward. As we descend, the stairway widens. Eventually we come out into a gargantuan chamber resonating with the sound of voices in disagreement. To my right is tiered seating carved from sunlight, filled with spirits of purity and beauty. To my left is an abyss of darkness brimming with fire, talons and misshapen abominations.

Astride a monstrous dais in the centre of the chamber two huge beings sit in facing thrones. They exchange arguments, their voices as loud as storms, speaking a language I cannot understand. One is wreathed in light, his eye sockets a mass of lightning, the other is cloaked in night, her face a mask of flame.

Feeling smaller and more insignificant than I ever have before, I look up at Colin.

'This is the Chamber of Vindication,' says Colin, his voice just audible above the thundering voices.

'What am I supposed to do?'

'Do as you will.'

There is a new distance in Colin's voice. I feel I am on my own, as though something is expected of me, but I don't know what. Then I see a flaming ball arcing through the air like a whispering Spitfire. Its trajectory gives no definite idea if the parties of Light or Fire are responsible for throwing it.

I feel a sense of déjà vu as I run forward. There is no thought involved, no consideration. I'm simply doing what I must. Unlike the grenade in Kandahar, I see it with time to make a difference. I run towards the dais.

Angry voices boom around me. I see the flaming blob fly towards me. It isn't as big as I first thought, more the size of a melon than a fighter-plane. I throw myself on top of its molten mass. *Bang*.

I'm on my back, my body aflame with pain. Light and

Fire look down upon me. Both are frightening, yet magnificent to behold. Colin approaches, drawing their attention.

'Are you responsible for deploying the Devil's Crush?' spits the leader of Fire, no longer using the strange language of their arguments. Colin nods. 'You do not have the authority.'

'I did so at the bequest of my master,' says Colin.

'Who do you serve that has the right to—'

Colin clears his throat. Twin tongues of fire flicker from his nostrils. 'Nature.'

The demeanours of both Light and Fire change instantly and they bow.

'My apologies,' says Fire.

'Accepted,' says Colin.

'His actions show hope,' says the leader of the Light, looking back down at me after a moment of contemplation, 'as I have argued.'

'They do,' the leader of Fire concedes. 'So it is decided.'

The two beings move back to the dais and retake their seats. As my consciousness fades, an announcement is made from the fiery abyss to the left, in that alien language. Both leaders listen and then the thunderous arguments begin once more.

4

I wake in my bed, glad the nightmare is over. I roll out from under the sheets, remembering I don't have legs a second too late. Wallop. 'Tufted-twist-pile, tufted-twist-pile,' I mutter, hoping it might help me remember.

'Morning, Joshua,' Colin's voice rumbles from the

kitchen. So it wasn't a dream.

I pull myself into my wheelchair and trundle into the kitchen. He's watching the news, sitting on his iron chair. It's a story about how a change in seismic activity means Yellowstone's super-volcano is no longer expected to erupt imminently.

'I'm alive.'

He nods. 'Enjoy.'

'I have no legs.'

'How would you explain them if you did?'

I'd never thought of that, but, 'I'd find a way.'

Colin just shakes his head.

'What about my soul?' I ask.

'What about it?'

'I was hoping—'

'Should have read the small print,' says Colin.

I'm beginning to wish I had. We watch the news report for a while. Scientists seem confused, people seem pleased. 'Did I act as Nature intended?' I ask.

'You did as you did. There was no right or wrong outcome.' Standing, Colin says, 'However, your actions have merely postponed disaster. I hope your race is wise enough to do as you did, and make the necessary sacrifices.'

'What can I do?' I ask.

I receive Colin's smouldering stare one last time. 'What can anyone do?'

Then he, his chair and the stench of flame are gone.

I feel different. It takes me a while to realise it's nothing physical. My thoughts are positive. What can I do with my life? How can I make a difference? As I put the kettle on, for the first time I find myself considering how I can best lead a life without legs.

~

ALTERNATIVE AFTERLIVES

THE NINJA ZOMBIE KNITTING CIRCLE

Heavy, infrequent droplets of rain began to pelt from an inky sky as Detective Inspector Eric Carter parked his car outside number seven, Cedar Walk. He ran under the overhang of the porch just as the deluge became biblical.

The large house was set back from the road, surrounded by tall trees that swayed in the stormy gusts of wind. For burglars, this secluded property offered an ideal location to work, concealed in the safety of shadow.

Carter looked at his watch. It was approaching his most coveted time of day. Deep night, he called it. Two until three a.m. A time regarded as late at night rather than early in the morning, when the drunks were retiring and the milkmen were rising. Most people slept through the glory that night had to offer. It was the time of day when Carter felt most alive. Tonight, the rain brought an extra depth to the dark. The night felt close, like a protective cloak about his shoulders.

Savouring the taste of damp air and tree pollen, he rang the doorbell. It clanged. The door opened almost immediately, answered by the elderly lady who owned the house, as if she had been anticipating his visit. She wore a flowery dress, worthy of prime position in an Oxfam shop window. Her slipper-boots were fluffy, her grey hair smart, her eyes glinting with what Carter took to be mischief.

'I'm sorry to bother you at such an hour, Mrs Eckless.'

'Inspector Carter, how nice to see you again, dear. Do come in.'

Carter walked into a dated but pristine hallway. The wallpaper and carpet were a swirling mass of flowery patterns and gaudy colours from the 70s. The skirting and ceiling shone white in contrast. He removed his coat and hung it on the newel post at the bottom of the stairs.

'I was worried I'd wake you, Mrs Eckless.'

'Oh, there's no danger of that on a Tuesday, my dear,' the old lady replied. 'And do stop being so formal. My name's Ethel.'

Carter smiled his best policeman's smile. It was appropriate for any occasion, be it pleasant, awkward or disagreeable. He liked to believe it was unreadable.

'So, what is it that keeps you up so late on a Tuesday?' he asked.

'The ninja zombie knitting circle. We meet every week, without fail.'

There was a twinkle in Ethel's eyes that Carter didn't like. He'd been mistaken about mischief. It was a testing twinkle, like you find in the eyes of devout believers in God who are prying to see if you share their belief or if you need converting.

'That's an unusual name,' said Carter, challenging his judgement. Had he simply misread a joke?

'Not really,' said Ethel. 'You have to be a ninja or a zombie to join. Gladys is a ninja and Joan is a zombie.'

'Which are you?'

'Oh, I'm a little bit of both, my love.'

Carter had a lot of experience with people. He could read them, ascertain underlying hints in their character from the way they said and did things. And he was particularly adept at spotting lies. In this instance he had no doubt about one thing. Ethel believed her words were the truth.

Up until this point, Carter would have readily accepted a cup of tea, had it been offered, and maybe some cake or homemade biscuits. The house was spotless. Cleanliness ticked one box in Carter's list of rules for accepting hospitality. But the second box was mental stability. At the first sign of senility he would politely steer the conversation towards business, rather than doing his bit for community relations by risking imbibing poison via off milk or the dubious cake mixtures employed by the partially sighted and mentally unsound.

'It sounds like a very unusual and exciting knitting circle,' said Carter.

'Oh, it is, my dear, it is. Gladys and Joan are having a knit-off. We forget the time when war commences.'

The frenzied clack Carter could hear from behind the living room door suggested this particular knitting battle was likely to continue in rampant fashion until sunrise.

'Would you like a nice warm cocoa, dear?' asked Ethel. 'You must be freezing.'

'No thank you, Ethel, I don't want to intrude on your fun. I'm actually here because there've been two burglaries in the area and a neighbour has reported suspicious activity outside your house.'

'Do you think it's those people I reported last week?'

'I very much doubt it,' replied Carter, remembering his previous visit. It turned out that the robbery Ethel Eckless had reported was of the daylight variety. She'd received a bill from her energy supplier which she'd described as criminal. At that time, Carter had assumed the old lady to be entertainingly eccentric rather than demented.

'Did you manage to arrest them?' Ethel asked.

'British Gas? No.'

Ethel tutted. 'It's wicked what they do to my generation. Wicked.'

Carter nodded sympathetically. 'Is it OK if I take a look around the house?'

'Yes, dear, yes. You do whatever you need to do. I'll put the kettle on.'

'There's really no need.'

'I insist, dear, I insist.'

She waddled off towards the kitchen. Carter decided to start upstairs. He was careful to make a thorough sweep of the house, looking in every room. It was no surprise that he found no one else in the property, no open windows, no broken locks. Just more wallpaper that would benefit from extinction and furniture that would make an antique dealer's heart palpitate. Using a step ladder he found in the third bedroom, he put his head into the loft and shone his torch around. All was quiet, save for the whistling of the wind around the eaves and the patter of raindrops on the tiles.

Back in the kitchen, he found the back door locked, the three point locking mechanism working perfectly. Again, all the windows were closed and locked. And next to the kettle was a steaming mug of cocoa, surrounded by an artistic arrangement of custard creams. He picked up the cocoa and moved back down the hallway before knocking on the living room door and opening it.

Inside, he found two elderly ladies sitting side by side on the sofa behind a whirlwind of knitting needles and brightly coloured wool. Arthritis seemed to have been thwarted by these two dextrous women. One wore a dress similar to Ethel's. Her skin had a plastic sheen, as though she might be an animated Madame Tussauds' waxwork. The other wore a black shinobi shozoko, complete with balaclava, and had a sword strapped to her back. Ethel was sitting in a chair opposite them with a stopwatch in one hand and a cup of tea in the other. She looked up as Carter entered the room.

'Ah, good, you found your cocoa, dear. That'll warm you up.'

'Yes, thank you.'

The other two women kept clacking away, ignoring him completely, their focus unbroken.

'Any sign of a break-in?' asked Ethel.

'No, nothing,' said Carter. He eyed the lip of the mug in his hands. It was clean, with no sign of lipstick or tea stains. He decided to risk a sip, and then nodded at his host appreciatively. 'Do you remember I looked around the house when I was here last week, gave it a quick safety inspection?'

'Yes, dear,' said Ethel, who had returned to studying the competition on the sofa intently. 'That was very kind of you.'

Carter took a gulp of cocoa. 'I remember noticing a particularly elegant necklace hanging from the mirror in your bedroom,' he said.

'Yes, dear.'

'Have you moved it?'

'No, dear. It lives on the mirror. I never move it.'

'I'm afraid it's gone.'

The words Carter had spoken brought an instant end to the knit-off. The clacking and thrashing of needles stopped so abruptly that an eerie silence filled the room. Carter had the full attention of the three women. There was something rather unnerving about their attentiveness, as though the scrutiny in their eyes might open doors in Carter's mind that he'd prefer to remain shut.

'Gone?'

Carter nodded gravely.

'I thought you said there was no sign of a break-in? How can my necklace be missing if no one broke in?'

There was an accusing timbre in Ethel's voice, which put Carter on edge. His gut was telling him there was something wrong with this situation, but he couldn't quite decide what.

Carter licked his lips. 'Have you had any roofing work done lately?'

'Yes. Yes, I have,' Ethel replied. 'A few days after your last visit, a young man came to my door and asked if I wanted a free roof inspection.'

'Did you accept?'

'I did, dear, I did. He had a look and said the roof was fine, but I had a few loose tiles. Seeing as he already had his ladder in place, would I like him to fix them.'

Carter nodded knowingly. This was the answer he knew he'd receive. 'We've been tracking a burglar now for a while. Part of his MO—'

'His what, dear?'

'His MO, his modus operandi. Thieves develop a routine, a pattern that becomes consistent and identifies them.'

'I see, Inspector Carter, I see.'

The way Ethel used his name made butterflies flap in Carter's stomach. Old ladies, even those with an interesting take on reality, should not seem this threatening. There was an inexplicable tension in the room, and in Carter's body. Over the years, he'd learned to rely on his intuition. It was seldom wrong. Right now, it screamed at him to get out. Rather than being abrupt, he decided to politely explain his theory, offer his cousin Keith's services to fix the roof, and leave as quickly as he could.

'A roofer always visits the property a few days before the robbery,' said Carter. 'They put fake tiles in place that are works of art, because they look real, but actually create an easy to open doorway into your attic space. It just slides open at a touch.'

Ethel and Zombie Joan gave each other a knowing glance. Ninja Gladys's rheumy eyes were transfixed on Carter, glaring from behind her balaclava.

'Then the robber waits for a particularly dark night, like tonight,' Carter continued, 'and climbs onto the roof, through the door into your loft, down the loft hatch, rifles through your things, takes what he wants and leaves the same way. I'll bet that if I climb into your loft space and give it close inspection, I'll find a door in the roof. I'm afraid you've been burgled by the Rooftop Phantom.'

'Never trust a skinny cook,' said Ethel Eckless.

'I'm sorry,' said Carter, thrown by the sudden retort. He felt dizzy and flopped back into an empty armchair, dropping his drink.

'Fat cooks like the food they prepare, dear,' said Ethel, her bones clicking as she pulled herself out of her seat and waddled towards him. 'You always know you'll receive a good meal from a fat cook. But you can't trust a skinny cook, dear. That's why I poisoned your cocoa.'

'What?'

'Let me guess what happens next. You'll suggest sending a roofer around, probably a friend of yours,

31

who will charge me a very reasonable rate to fix my roof. Is that right, dear?'

Carter felt sick. He didn't answer. He just sat there, wondering if Ethel really had poisoned him. He'd totally misread her.

'You steal my necklace and then you make money out of me by fixing a roof that doesn't need fixing. Twice. Once before you rob me, once after. Am I right?' Not waiting for Carter's reply, Ethel continued, 'I was suspicious after your last visit. There was something contrived about your offer of a safety check. And this proves me right. A policeman with all the answers, dear, he's like a skinny cook. The story he tells is like a bad meal: tasteless and unpalatable. You're tricky, but I see you, dear, I see you clearly. And your story is inedible.'

Carter felt anxiety crawl through him. Did Ethel Eckless plan to kill him? This was beginning to feel like a nightmare, where everything had become sticky and some invisible force was clawing at him, slowing him down, making it impossible to scream.

'Be a dear and empty your pockets, Inspector Carter.'

'No,' said Carter, giving his best policeman's smile. This was ridiculous. He was an officer of the law. Why should he feel threatened by three old ladies who were jumping to conclusions? It's not like they were drug dealers with guns. There was nothing to be scared of.

He went to stand. Nothing happened. His limbs simply didn't respond. He tried again and noticed an emotionless smile resting on Ethel's lips.

'Have you really poisoned me?' he asked.

'Oh yes, dear. That's why you can't move. The paralysis will slowly creep up your neck. Soon, you'll struggle to speak.'

'This has gone far enough, Ethel. Call me an ambulance.'

Ethel didn't move. Carter noticed that her eyes had become hardened and cool. Little icebergs had risen all over her personality. Behind her, Ninja Gladys rose from the sofa with an easy grace that belied her age. She moved towards him and began to go through his pockets. Of course, she found nothing.

'We've been hunting this criminal for months now, Mrs Eckless. Months,' said Carter. 'We're so close to catching him. That's because we've found answers after lots of police work. Really, we're this close.' He went to raise his arm, intending to indicate just how near they were by gesturing with thumb and forefinger held millimetres apart. He couldn't move.

'Go and look through his jacket, would you Joan?' said Ethel.

Zombie Joan pushed herself up from the sofa and shuffled into the hall.

'You're not going to find anything,' said Carter. 'You're making a huge mistake.'

Joan returned and shook her head. For the first time, Carter noticed doubt in Ethel Eckless's eyes. 'You're all going to be in lots of trouble,' he said, using a calm voice filled with reason. 'I'm just here to help you, Ethel. Please, call me an ambulance.'

He was about to go on when he noticed Gladys eyeing his shoes suspiciously. She bent down, untied his laces and pulled the shoes from his feet.

'This is ridiculous, ladies,' he said. 'One of you has to call me a doctor.'

'Do shut up, dear,' said Ethel, making four softly spoken words sound like a death threat. Doubt had vacated her eyes.

Gladys toyed with Carter's shoes. After a few moments of studying them, the ninja placed her fingers around the heel of the left shoe, expertly locating the correct pressure points. The heel slid clear. Ethel's necklace dropped from its hiding place to rest on the carpet, shimmering seductively. Carter had guessed it must be worth thousands. A tear welled in his eye. His instinct was overwhelming – his life had never been in so much jeopardy.

'I have debts,' he said. 'My daughter, she's ill. A policeman's salary won't cover my needs. I know it's not an excuse, but it's a reason why I acted in this appalling manner.'

'You're not good at lying, my love,' said Ethel. 'You gamble and you lose, because you think you have a good poker face and an unreadable smile. You don't, dear. Not in the slightest.'

Carter realised he'd been caught, outwitted and outdone. How had he been so blind? Surely he couldn't be that easy to read, he'd been doing this for years. No, Ethel had just been lucky. He could still manipulate the situation and save himself.

'Please forgive me,' he said, satisfied with the emotion he'd driven behind these words, making them sound genuine. 'I'm truly sorry for my actions.'

'The problem with Joan being a zombie is finding her enough food,' said Ethel. 'Fresh brains are so hard to come by.'

'Joan isn't a zombie, Ethel,' said Carter. His lips were tingling and he had to fight to speak. 'Zombies don't exist. Please, call an—'

'And the problem with being part-zombie myself,' interrupted Ethel, 'is that my ability to tell right from wrong has become blurred. It's like a distant memory I can't quite reach. But we do try to feed on those who deserve to be eaten.'

These women are mad, thought Carter. *Totally and utterly lost.*

He noticed Joan shuffling forwards, a small trickle of saliva on her waxy chin and a ravenous hunger in her dead eyes. She smiled, revealing black teeth and putrid gums.

'No,' he whispered.

'You won't feel a thing, dear,' said Ethel. 'The poison seems to be working a little too slowly, so Gladys will ensure you're unconscious before Joan tucks in.'

True to the nightmare he found himself in, Carter tried to scream, but no sound came from his mouth. Gladys leant over him and applied pressure to his neck. The last thought of Eric Carter's life surprised him.

Who'd have thought that ninjas and zombies liked to knit?

~

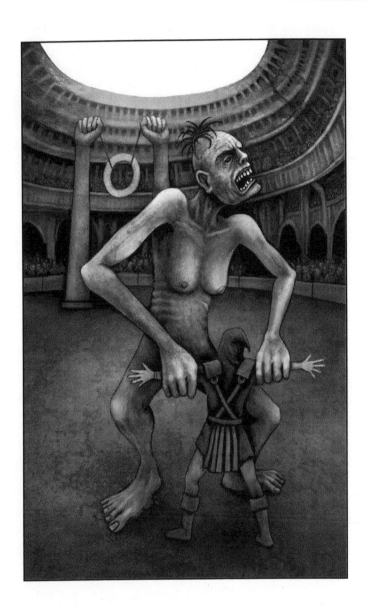

TROLL'S HEAD

1

Today Rage face death. Rage scared. Rage alive. Rage walk tunnel. Tunnel stinks. Cages line tunnel. Small cages. Iron bars. Trolls in cages. Rage bow to trolls.

War is great troll. Greatest troll. My man-troll. Tears in War's eyes. No room to bow.

War nod to Rage. Rage is War's wife-troll.

Team trolls stamp feet. Once. Together.

Team trolls shout, 'RAGE.' Once. Together.

Team trolls nod to Rage. Together. They know her power. Her plan. Rage brave. Today Rage die.

Whip crack. Blood trickle. Rage smile.

Rage walk to gate. Hear rain. Rain pour. Hear crowd. Crowd roar. Crowd lust. Crowd want game. Crowd want gore.

Fists clench. Rage ready. No more slave. Rage bring war.

2

Arbitrator Tiberius Horst disliked the great city of Seven Hills. The metropolis was vast, its sprawling streets alive with plots and corruption. It was everything he'd fought hard for his home, the fortified town of Willow Syx, not to become. Yet here he was, in the great city's coliseum, about to watch a game of blood.

The rain poured and cold gusts of wind whipped beneath the royal canopy. Horst could see blue sky on the horizon, and a distant rainbow. The view gave him hope. Collecting his thoughts, the arbitrator focussed on the real reason for his visit. All he had to do was tolerate the company of the monarch for a short while longer.

Horst glanced over at his host. Dressed in royal garb of red and gold, Potentate Maldras exuded regal authority. The ruler's looks were spoiled by an inflamed scar, which ran down the left side of his face from forehead to jaw, and eyes that were cold and scheming. Two stunning women lounged next to him on soft pillows, their silk clothing concealing nothing.

'Your slaves are cold,' said Horst. 'They're shivering.'

'But they're beautiful,' replied Maldras. 'It would be wrong of me to hide their bodies from my guests.'

'Their lips are blue.'

'Do not worry yourself, Tiberius. If they become too cold to satisfy your desires, I shall call for more.'

'You misunderstand me, sire. I do not like to see them suffer.'

'Then do not look at them.'

Horst sensed Maldras relishing his discomfort. There was an inherent cruelty about the man. With this warmonger on the throne of Gordesia, peace wouldn't prevail; Horst's efforts to make Willow Syx a place of safety and prosperity could never endure.

'Here, lady,' said Horst, addressing the slave to Maldras's right, 'take my cloak.'

The slave looked at the floor.

'You are in Seven Hills begging the aid of my army, Arbitrator Horst,' said Maldras, 'and you insult me by disrespecting my hospitality. Would you prefer that I ignore your pleas and let the town of Willow Syx burn?'

Maldras's words were delivered with the cool indifference of diplomacy, while his eyes shone with wickedness. Inwardly, Horst chided his own stupidity; he had to make more effort to hide his disgust. If Maldras were to guess the true reason behind Horst's visit, months of careful planning would be wasted.

'I apologise, sire,' said Horst. 'Please, forgive me. I have a weakness for women that leads me to speak before consulting my commonsense.'

Maldras nodded approvingly. 'Apology accepted, Tiberius. You have a way with words that I find amusing.'

'You are most gracious, sire.'

Horst looked out over the coliseum. It was vast, constructed from red rock quarried east of the city in the foothills of the Gordesian Mountains. The coliseum's turfed pitch was a sodden quagmire. Two pillars stood at each end of the arena, carved to represent gigantic fists emerging from the soil. Hanging vertically between each pair of fists was a massive circle of stone suspended some 30 feet in the air from thick ropes.

A gong sounded and the crowd surged to their feet. Horst saw a door open on the opposite side of the arena. From it emerged a huge warrior dressed in burnished leather armour. The crowd began to chant, 'Butcher, Butcher, Butcher,' as he strode onto the pitch. Once at the centre of the arena, drenched by the rain, the warrior knelt and wiped mud from the floor onto his face. Pulling an executioner's hood over his head, he stood and raised his arms to the crowd. They roared in approval.

The gong sounded again. A grinding noise rumbled

through the foundations of the coliseum. Horst saw the arena floor shake. From beneath the mud and grass, a blood-stained stone slowly erupted into view. A colossal axe rested against it. The executioner hefted the weapon as the aged gate at the end of the arena slowly opened. The noise from the crowd began to crescendo.

Beyond the gate, inky shadows lingered. Horst could sense something looming in the darkness, its unseen presence feeding the frenzy of the gathered masses.

3

Gate old. Carved. Made by humans. Humans make pretty. Humans make ugly. Rage not understand humans.

Whip Man open gate. Whip Man cruel. Whip Man think Rage stupid.

One whip. One guard. One troll. Whip Man stupid.

'Go to the Butcher, bitch,' Whip Man say. Whip Man spits on Rage.

Rage use shadow. Rage grab Whip Man neck. Whip Man struggle. Rage squeeze. Whip Man snap. Rage lay Whip Man body in shadow. Rage whisper Trolls' Prayer. Whip Man soul fly free.

Rage stand. Rage walk through gate. Walk in rain. Walk on pitch. See Axe Man. Crowd jeer.

Rage shout, 'RAGE.'

Rage throw mud at Axe Man. Axe Man stumble. Axe Man fall.

Crowd cheer. Rage bow. Crowd cheer more. Rage know, they still want gore.

4

Horst watched in awe as the troll walked from the shadows. She was colossal, at least 15 feet tall, with enormous shoulders and arms that hung to the floor. Her skin was mud-brown and leathery, her face ugly, her eyes dark and menacing. A tuft of thick hair sprouted from the crown of her head, on the spot where a man might go bald. Trolls were widely regarded as slow and clumsy due to their bulk, but this monster walked with effortless grace.

'Is the game easy to follow?' asked Horst, feigning interest.

'Its simplicity is its beauty,' replied Maldras. 'The objective is to achieve the highest number of goals. A goal is scored each time the ball passes through one of the hanging circles of stone. How they are scored or defended is left entirely to the ingenuity and power of each team.'

As the troll walked towards the centre of the pitch and the waiting Butcher, the crowd jeered mockingly. The troll raised a fist to the sky and bellowed, 'RAGE.' Then it pounded its fist into the floor with a wet thud. Taking a clod of earth in its fist, the troll flung mud at the Butcher with such force that he lost his balance, falling to the ground.

The crowd responded with a cheer and Horst saw the troll bow.

'What is the significance of 'rage'?' asked Horst.

'The troll is shouting its name,' said Maldras. There was a new menace in the potentate's tone, as though the reaction of the crowd were an insult to his ears. 'It's what they do before they die.'

'I'm sorry, sire, I don't fully understand the rules.

Willow Syx is distant and we hear conflicting stories regarding the sport.'

'The troll is to be killed. Its head will be cut off by the Butcher and then used as the ball in the coming game.'

'Forgive me, sire, but that seems barbaric, and beneath your majesty.'

Maldras nodded. 'In some ways you are right, Tiberius. But barbarity ensures the greatness of the sport. The troll that gives the poorest performance in any game is sacrificed at the next. This simple rule makes every player give their all. The strongest survive and the game becomes greater each time it is played. It's what makes Troll's Head so compelling, so addictive. The savagery of the game feeds the public spirit. It allows me to keep control.'

'Your sense of right and wrong seems lost, potentate.'

'Do not allow your tongue too much freedom, Arbitrator Horst. These are trolls we talk of. I find your insolence tiresome.'

'My humblest apologies, sire. The excitement of the coming game has made me forget the nobility of my company.'

'Accepted, Tiberius. For the last time.'

5

Axe Man big. Big man like baby troll.

Axe Man get up. Axe Man angry. Points at Great Game Stone.

'Kneel,' Axe Man say. 'Give your head to the game.'

'No,' Rage say.

'This is an honour none of your kind deserve,' Axe

Man say. 'Accept it with grace, troll.'

'Axe Man want Rage head,' Rage shout, 'Axe Man take Rage head.'

Crowd cheer. Axe Man angry. Axe Man swing axe.

One axe. One man. One troll. Axe Man stupid.

Rage block axe. Axe Man stumble. Rage grab Axe Man arms. Rage pull. Axe man scream. Arms come off. Rage throw Axe Man arms at crowd.

Crowd roar. Crowd happy. Crowd got gore.

6

Devilry danced in Maldras's eyes as the Butcher's right arm thudded against the stone floor, spraying blood onto his courtiers. The crowd were bellowing Rage's name over and over. 'How dare they celebrate this show of disrespect,' he said.

'The people admire the troll's bravery, potentate,' said Horst. Before he could get a grip on his tongue, he finished, 'As do I.'

Maldras turned to face Horst. 'My elite guard tell me traitors have been breaking into the holding cells beneath the coliseum, Tiberius, and holding audience with the trolls.'

'That is troubling news, sire,' Horst replied smoothly. 'Why would anyone do that?'

'I've also received conflicting reports from my informants. Some verify that Willow Syx is threatened by an army of renegades, but some suggest the town is in no danger at all. They bring news of traitors plotting assassinations and mutiny.'

'Willow Syx lies many miles west, sire. Reports travel via a string of informants. They become twisted. It's often hard to discern truth from hearsay.'

'True, Tiberius, but the combination of these reports and your displays of open disrespect disconcert me. They arouse my suspicions and I find myself questioning your loyalty.'

'I understand, majesty, and apologise if I've appeared rude. It is not my intention. My mind is filled with worry for my people and it's affecting my judgement. I am, and will always be, your loyal subject.'

'It would put my mind at rest if you would prove your allegiance.'

'Of course, lord. I'll do anything you ask.'

Maldras gestured towards the pitch. 'Deal with this inconvenience for me, Tiberius.'

'Sire?'

'The game cannot be played without a ball.'

Horst felt uneasy. This would ruin everything. 'Tradition dictates that you should accompany your elite guards to face the troll in such a situation, lord. Are you sure it's wise to deprive the crowd of such a spectacle when they seem so agitated?'

'You appear to have a greater understanding of the rules than you led me to believe.' Horst saw a cruel smile on Maldras's lips. 'It's as though you want me to stand before that troll, Tiberius, a beast blessed with agility and gifted in the art of murder. Imagine if it killed me before my guards could react. What might an event like that invoke? A riot? An uprising?'

Horst just stared at Maldras, vexed by his own idiocy.

'The men you sent to free the trolls of the 10 teams are dead,' said Maldras. 'Your plots are crumbling. As a traitorous ringleader, I feel it fitting that you are forced to take the life of your ally.'

Despite his feelings for Maldras, Horst had to admire his cunning. Hearing their leader had killed Rage would seed speculation and mistrust within the resistance, weakening unity. 'And if I refuse?' he asked.

'The people of Willow Syx will suffer military rule from my mercenary army while they hunt your co-conspirators. As you know, mercenaries do not possess the same level of discipline or decency as my elite guard.'

That was an understatement. Horst stood. 'You leave me little choice,' he said.

'I must know one thing,' said Maldras. 'How did you intend to control so many trolls? There is a reason I only allow 20 onto the pitch at a time.'

'I did not seek to control them. I planned to fight alongside them. Together we would've fought for peace.'

'Idealism is a wretched weakness, Tiberius.'

With a click of the fingers, Maldras summoned his nearest guards. As Horst was escorted to the pitch, Maldras called after him, 'Be sure to put on a good show, Tiberius. The lives of your people depend on it.'

7

ate open. Horst walk out. Walk in rain. Walk in mud. No weapon. Pretty clothes.

Gate close. Horst not Maldras. Plan wrong.

'The 100 trolls of the 10 teams will remain caged,' Horst say. 'I've been sent to take your head.'

'Plan broken,' Rage say. 'Die for nothing.'

'I still see a chance,' Horst say.

Horst act mad. Point finger. Shout at Rage. Put on

show.

Crowd jeer. Horst clever.

'Crowd jeer man,' Rage say. 'Crowd cheer troll. People angry.'

Horst nod. 'There's a fervour brewing that I dared not wish for. The people crave an end to tyranny. Your defiance has inspired them. We still have a chance to start the uprising.'

'How?'

'I have a plan, but it has little chance of success.'

'Tell Rage.'

Horst act angry, tell plan fast. Rage like plan. Horst give Rage hope. Horst good man. Horst friend.

'Rage give them show,' Rage say. 'Rage give them gore. Rage make them rise. Rage start a war.'

8

A back handed blow sent Horst spinning through the air. He landed heavily, sliding through the filth of the pitch. Rage hadn't held back. Good. This had to look real.

As Horst hauled himself to his feet, he heard the frenzy of the crowd. Rage roared her name, playing to the masses, feeding their hysteria. Horst glanced up, considering the barbed spikes that jutted from the stone base of the royal enclosure like a protective crown. Could Rage clear them? He must give her the chance to try.

Horst walked over to the Butcher's fallen axe. There was no doubt in his mind. He'd witnessed the potentate's false promises too many times. Maldras would send the mercenary army into Willow Syx regardless. Horst had nothing to lose.

Hefting the weapon from the sodden ground, Horst drew the attention of the crowd by striding to the centre of the arena, as if to make a last heroic stand. He glanced up at the rows of archers and spearmen who stood ready to rain death on the arena floor if there were trouble during the game. He hoped that he could draw their gaze, just long enough to give Rage her chance.

Removing his cloak and shirt, Horst turned to face the royal box. He pulled the blade of the axe across his chest, drawing a thin line of blood. This aged ritual, conducted by warriors proud to be selected to fight to the death by their king, stirred the clamour of the crowd further.

Horst saw that Rage had moved closer to the arena wall, playing the part of a predator circling its prey, awaiting the perfect moment to strike. Her eyes were on him.

Horst raised his arms to the sky and bellowed. He could do no more to draw attention away from the troll. He hoped Rage would recognise this as her signal to strike.

She did.

Horst watched in awe as the troll launched herself at the arena wall. The royal enclosure was situated 50 feet above the ground. A combination of Rage's height, reach and power allowed her to leap and grasp one of the massive spikes. Despite the pain the barbs must have caused, she swung herself up into the royal enclosure in one lithe movement.

Horst saw archers taking aim, but Rage had landed directly in front of the potentate. If they missed the troll, they risked hitting royalty or honoured courtiers.

Many of them hesitated. Only a handful of arrows were loosed – too few to bring down a troll.

Beneath the golden canopy, soldiers reacted, drawing swords and running, but they were on the edges of the royal enclosure. It would take them valuable seconds to reach the monarch.

Rage had her opportunity.

Horst saw the troll lunge at Maldras. Grabbing his head in one of her fists, she tore it from his neck. Rage threw the head towards the far end of the arena. It bounced from the edge of one of the huge goals and passed through the circle of stone.

The crowd were roaring. A fresh level of vehemence was apparent in their cries. Soldiers were nervous. They drew weapons. Fights started. The revolt began.

Horst looked back at the royal enclosure and felt his elation falter. Rage was surrounded by guards, their swords a mass of slashing movement.

9

Rage think of War. War is great troll. Greatest troll. My man-troll.

Rage is War's wife-troll. Tears in Rage's eyes.

Rage turn to crowd. Rage cry, 'RAGE.'

Rage see Horst. Horst happy. We won. Horst sad. Rage gone.

Rage bow to Horst.

Swords stab. Swords cut. More gore.

Crowd not happy. Crowd rise. Crowd start war.

10

As Rage fell, Tiberius Horst fought back his regret. The time for contemplation and guilt would be later. Now, he must ensure Rage's sacrifice was worthwhile.

Rather than running, he walked with purpose towards the gate that led to the trolls' prison, hoping his act would be convincing enough to fool the archers. If they didn't yet know him as a traitor, they would simply have witnessed a heroic arbitrator facing a troll for his potentate.

The archers ignored him, concentrating their fire on the violence within the crowd, further infuriating the masses, fuelling the growing mania of the revolt. The sheer numbers of people were overpowering the soldiers.

Horst ran through the ancient gate and down a long, curving tunnel. Below the coliseum, he made his way to the cages that housed the trolls of the 10 teams. The usual squad of soldiers guarding this area were absent, probably drawn away by the commotion. Two guards were standing with their backs to Horst at the foot of a stairwell, their attention on the sounds of battle echoing down from above. Using the weight of the Butcher's axe, Horst began smashing locks. By the time the two guards reacted, too many trolls were free.

11

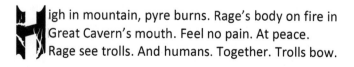

High in mountain, pyre burns. Rage's body on fire in Great Cavern's mouth. Feel no pain. At peace. Rage see trolls. And humans. Together. Trolls bow.

Humans bow.

'Rage died with the greatest of honour,' Horst say.

'War proud,' War say. Fight tears. 'Rage bravest of trolls.'

Horst nod. 'There will be more blood to come,' he say. 'More loss, more gore, more pain, more war.' Horst talk in Rage rhymes. He look sad.

'Hope of peace now alive,' War say. 'Rage gave this hope. You gave this hope. Now future has hope. World is better place.'

Horst bow to War. 'You are the wisest of leaders,' he say.

War say Trolls' Prayer. Rage's soul fly free. See path in sky. Stars beckon.

Rage look back.

War stand with Horst. Trolls stand with men. Men respect trolls.

These are new days.

~

ALTERNATIVE AFTERLIVES

THE EL PASO PHANTOM FEEDER

1

An unseasonal storm was throwing a fit the night I found myself seeking shelter in an El Paso hellhole called The Schmuck's Ruin. Rain lashed, wind whipped and thunder... well... thundered.

The Ruin looked like it belonged in a horror movie, but I was wetter than a mermaid's snatch, so I ignored my instincts and pushed the door open. There was only one other person sitting at the bar when I entered – a grizzled old guy, big as a bear. He didn't look up, just sat there, knocking back shots, staring at nothing.

'What do you have to do to get served in this shithole?' I asked.

Old Bear glanced at me. 'What you drinkin', lady?' His voice was deep, with a smoker's rasp.

'Whiskey.'

Old Bear leaned over the bar, helped himself to a drink like he owned the place and slid the glass towards me. I took off my coat, placed a few dollars on the bar and watched Old Bear, sipping my whiskey. Was he the man I'd been hunting for?

I was about to try starting a conversation when two young redneck pieces of shit stumbled in through the door. They had a dangerous look, their laughter false and attitude menacing. Pretending to scratch my leg, I unfastened the securing strap on the holster hidden inside my boot, removed the gun and tucked it into my jeans for easy access.

One of the rednecks sat next to Old Bear and prodded his arm with a grimy finger.

'Howdy, ol' cuss,' he said. 'You wanna party?'

Old Bear ignored him.

'Why'd you hang out here? This place is a fuckin' hole.'

Old Bear shrugged.

'Full o' fuckin' ass lovin' shit lickers.'

Old Bear nodded.

'You like ass, ol' timer? Smells like you do. Smells like you fuckin' love it.'

Old Bear went back to ignoring him.

'What's up, ol' man? I just messin' with you, havin' some fun. Why you bein' such a dick?' He looked at his buddy, who seemed unable to take his dilated eyeballs off my tits, and they both laughed laughs that weren't laughs. 'I done somethin' to upset your dumb ass?'

'Leave me be, kid,' said Old Bear. 'I ain't good company.'

'Oh shit, ol' cuss. I just bein' friendly. What the fuck's your problem?' As he said this, the redneck prodded Old Bear again.

'I got no problem, kid, it's all you.' For the first time, Old Bear looked up. His eyes twinkled with controlled anger. 'Now leave me be.'

The redneck stood and knocked the drink from Old Bear's hand with a childish slap. 'You wanna take this outside, ol' man?'

'Sure thing, kid.'

As Old Bear stood up I realised he was even bigger than I'd first thought. He took off his denim jacket, revealing tattooed arms, decorated with demons, devils and hellfire, and a pendant hanging around his neck on a chain. It depicted a woman nailed to an inverted crucifix. He folded the denim and placed it on the bar.

Sticks and stones looked like they'd have to be hurled by the Incredible Hulk to hurt Old Bear, so names stood no chance. Still, the two rednecks goaded him with puerile insults as they walked towards the door.

As they made their way outside, the one who'd had his eyes super-glued to my tits paused in the doorway, turned back and said, 'When we done with him, we comin' to play with you, pretty bitch.'

I blew him a kiss and said, 'Can't wait.'

My lack of fear must've annoyed him — I saw a glower set on his sweaty face. 'I'm gonna enjoy hurtin' you.' The redneck drew a knife from his pocket, grinned, and disappeared out of the door.

To this day, I don't know what happened outside The Schmuck's Ruin, but a few minutes later Old Bear walked back in, put his jacket on and poured himself another drink. Rain dripped from his greying hair and a shallow cut decorated his forehead. Aside from that, he was exactly as before.

I noticed a killer's coldness lingering in Old Bear's eyes. My hunt might be over.

'You talk them down?' I asked.

'Somethin' like that,' he said.

'They coming back?'

'I doubt it, lady.' He took a swig of liquor. 'You Australian?'

'English.'

'Don't get many limeys in these parts.'

'That's why I like it,' I lied.

We sat for a while in companionable silence. When

I'd finished my whiskey, I said, 'What you drinking?'

'Panty Peeler,' Old Bear replied.

'What's a Panty Peeler?'

'Try one and see.'

I did. I wished I hadn't. It looked like water and burned like a bad chili relleno.

'Tastes like shit,' I said.

'And your panties are still on.' He gave me a wicked wink. 'Better have another.'

I took his advice. By the time I'd had my second, I found myself craving a third and swearing like I had Tourette's.

'You talk like a guy,' said Old Bear.

'Think like one too. Make you uncomfortable?'

He shook his head. 'It's unusual.'

'My parents died and I was raised by my brothers. Got a man's mouth and a woman's body.'

As we drank, me and Old Bear got talking, starting with small bites of crap, moving on to bigger chunks of bullshit. His name was Cyrus McGruder and he owned the Schmuck's Ruin. To my surprise, I found myself liking him. He had a dry sense of humour and a no shit attitude. Not that it mattered. If he was the murdering son of a bitch I guessed him to be, McGruder was mine. I was long overdue a payday and the bounty on a serial killer would sort my finances for a year or more.

'You haven't told me your name,' McGruder said, after returning from a piss break.

'Scarlett Blaine,' I said.

'What you doin' in this shithole, Scarlett Blaine?'

'I'm a journalist.'

'Journalist, eh?' He didn't sound like he believed me. Well he sure as shit wouldn't have guessed my real profession. Your stereotypical bounty hunter doesn't have my physique. I sound bigger than I look.

'I'm investigating the disappearances,' I said.

'What disappearances?'

'Every few years, during storms, people go missing.'

'First I've heard of it.'

'Usually vagrants, people no one would miss.'

'So why give a shit?'

'Someone has to, Cyrus.'

McGruder shrugged and stood up. There was a new distance in his eyes.

'Smoke?' he asked.

Foolishly, I said, 'Yeah, I'd love one.'

2

utside, the rain came down like Niagara and bursts of lightning shredded the shadows. We stood under the porch. McGruder lit a cigarette and passed it to me, then lit one for himself. There was no sign of the rednecks – no sign of anyone.

'You know what I think?' he said.

'Telepathy isn't my thing.'

'You're prettier than you are clever.' The way he spoke made my skin tingle.

'Well, you're older than you are wise.'

'Touché, Scarlett Blaine.' He took a quick step towards me.

Crying like a jittery bitch isn't my style. I went for my gun.

Moving with speed I hadn't expected, McGruder grabbed my wrist before my fingers could touch the pistol-grip. I tried to slam my knee into his groin, but he sidestepped and shoved me into the wall, winding me.

Before I could refill my lungs, he pressed something into my forehead. It burned so bad I screamed, but the noise was lost in the storm. I felt numbness spreading through me. McGruder took a step back and, as I fell over, I saw the inverted crucifix dangling from his hand. It glowed like fire.

'What have you done to me?' I asked. It was a struggle to enunciate the words – my tongue felt like a swollen slug.

'Marked you as ghost fodder.' I saw a look of genuine remorse on his face. 'Sorry, Scarlett Blaine, I ain't got no choice. I have to feed her, or my soul's forfeit.'

'Gutless fuck.'

I guess he'd been called worse. He just nodded and said, 'Most people are paralysed by her brand. You got fire enough to fight it, but take an old man's advice. When the phantom comes, don't resist her. It'll be a whole lot worse if you do.'

3

As McGruder walked back inside the Ruin, I floundered on the porch, trying to stand on legs that wouldn't do as I commanded. I slipped and smacked my head on the floor. Fuck. This couldn't be happening.

As I tried to will my limbs into sorting their shit out, the storm tugged at my clothing and clawed at my skin as if it were coming to life. I felt invisible hands gripping my shoulders. They turned me, slamming me onto my back. Hearing a disgusting suckling noise, I watched a shadow take physical form in front of me.

A figure appeared, standing above me. It swayed back and forth, its long black robe sodden with rain.

'What the fuck are you?' I managed to ask, despite the state of my tongue.

It just stood there, swaying, but I discerned a whisper on the wind.

Phantom.

Lightning flashed repeatedly in the distance, banishing the shadows just enough to illuminate the creature. It was a woman, but she looked like a half-hearted imitation of a human, as though someone had sculpted her but lost interest before completing the project, leaving her to rot. Her eyes were red and lidless, her mouth black and slimy, her skin pallid and papery. There was something cruel about the way she watched me, a pitiless look writhing in her eyes and a smirk shrouding her wet mouth. It lacked any compassion or morality.

Never knowing when to shut my mouth, I said, 'Euthanasia's the only cure for that much ugly.'

The rancid smirk slithered from her lips and she lunged, clawing at my face. Her touch was cold and repulsive. Nausea engulfed me. I spewed vomit like I was at an audition for *The Exorcist*. She moved in quickly, her lips pulling back to reveal pointed teeth protruding from black gums.

I fought the numbness in my limbs, willing them to move. Somehow, I managed to lash out. My thumbs found her eyes. I pushed and they sank into her sockets, down to the knuckle.

Thank you, the wind whispered.

A light drifted from the phantom's mouth, travelling free on her final breath. For a second, I saw a woman's face shimmer above me. There were tears in her eyes.

As quickly as she'd appeared, she faded into the night.

The phantom's body started to crumble over me. Excruciating pain engulfed me. As I writhed and screamed I saw that my skin was rotting, my flesh decaying.

McGruder returned from inside the Ruin and stood on the porch, watching me.

A new pain erupted behind my eyes. It felt like something was eating my brain. 'Help me,' I pleaded.

'Can't.' He lit a cigarette. 'You fought her and won. The curse is yours now.'

I screamed as pain filled my skull.

'I warned you,' McGruder said.

The pain suddenly stopped.

I don't like being told. My voice was the wind, the wrath of the storm. *You'll feed me?*

McGruder nodded. 'I have to. I'm as cursed as you.'

I stood and felt the weight of a storm sodden cloak about my shoulders.

See you, McGruder.

'Soon, Scarlett Blaine,' replied the feeder. 'Too soon.'

The wind banshees shrieked and electricity split the sky with forks of death light. Drawn by the storm, I reached for the wind. And flew.

~

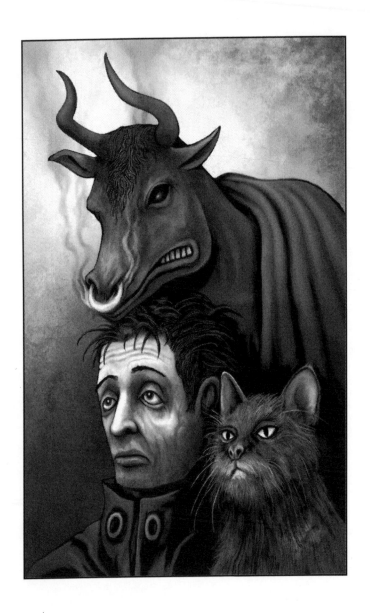

THE CAT, THE BULL AND THE MADMAN

Part One – The Cat

I'm awake, but I'm damned if I'm letting Mr Pooch in on the secret. Every morning is the same. According to Gwendolyn, my counsellor, settling into a routine will help my recovery, but when each day starts with a war of wills with a cat, it can't be healthy, especially when the cat is accustomed to victory.

I'd been enjoying a surreal dream. I was in a kitchen, watching an impossibly fat cook basting human heads on a baking tray. The heads were all chatting amiably about the manner in which they'd been murdered.

As the cook went to shove the heads back into the oven, she stumbled, wobbled like a Weeble, and the tray tumbled to the floor. The heads all laughed about her clumsiness as they bounced around. I found their laughter so infectious that I joined in, but my giggles boomed like cannon-fire. The cook swung to face me. She looked like an entire tug o' war team in one body with one thing on their conjoined minds – my complete annihilation.

As she charged at me, I drew a blade from my belt and, just as I was about to stab her, He appeared, malignant pleasure at my return written across His wicked face. His laughter rumbled and then...

...I woke up. A crushing sense of loss filled me as I

realised I'd been dreaming and had again deprived myself of the delight the night offers. In the past this feeling might have consumed me, until my hunger became impossible to control, leading me to seek His counsel in the darkness.

As I lay there, fighting despair, Mr Pooch jumped onto the bed, distracting me and, as always, saving me from this destructive thought path. But there's a small part of me that doesn't want to be saved. It's the cruel, night-craving part of me that knows it's dying and, in futile defiance, it encourages me to feign sleep.

Mr Pooch moves to sit on my chest, making a point of not purring. I find this disconcerting, for I know what's coming next. I wait, and... There it is. He's flicking my bottom lip with his paw. I fight not to react and eventually he stops. My lips are probably lacerated beyond recognition, but I'm pleased with myself. Usually his relentless lip flicking tactics are enough to defeat me.

I feel him spring off my chest and hear him prowling around the bed, as if considering his options. I wonder what he's planning...

Mr Pooch jumps back onto my chest and forces his paw between my lips, into my mouth. Then he just sits there, with his paw lodged in my gob. Despite being on the receiving end of this fiendish move, I find myself impressed with his ingenuity. Still, I'm not giving up. We both remain motionless for a while. Then, as if bored with awaiting the inevitable outcome, Mr Pooch flexes his claws. They dig into my tongue. In addition to the pain, a foul taste seeps forth. I fight not to gag, but remember that personal hygiene isn't high on Mr Pooch's list of priorities.

'A-ight,' I say, through a mouthful of fur, claw and

God knows what. Outwitted by a cat. Again. Healthy routine my arse. As I sit up, Mr Pooch gracefully sidesteps off my chest and sits on the duvet, subjecting me to a pitiless stare.

He's a smallish cat with grey hair. It could be lovely and long, but Mr Pooch only likes to lick one thing, and it isn't his fur. His coat has become so matted, he looks like a walking dreadlock. One of his eyes is yellow, the other a misty blue. It's so unnatural it looks like a special effect in a pirate movie.

'What time is it?' I ask.

'Same time it always is,' he says. 'Six in the a.m.'

I know he's trying to look after me, but I'm not a morning person. My problem is more apparent late at night, so I go to bed early, take a sedative and sleep through the troublesome hours. But still, 'Is six a.m. really necessary?'

'Routine is good, Brian.'

'What about taking the advice of a talking cat?'

'Don't make me hurt you.'

I admit defeat and swing my legs out of the bed.

'I'm hungry,' he says. 'Let's eat.'

I pull on my dressing gown and follow Mr Pooch downstairs, trying not to look at his posterior. There dangle clumps of matted fur, caked in evil.

I make breakfast. Cereal for me, tuna for Mr Pooch.

'So?' I ask. 'What's the plan?'

'Rest. Lots of it,' he says, licking his fishy lips.

'Boring.'

'You have your review tomorrow.'

'I know, but—'

'No buts. Honour thy mother, thy father and thy sanity.'

How many times have I heard him say this? Too

many, but he does so with good reason. In the past, I found it impossible to understand why anyone would want a firm grounding in reality. Now, I'm still a fan of escapism, but recognise that I used to take it too far. With Mr Pooch's help, I've come to realise that there's no harm in a little imagination in my routine. It's when said imagination goes to war with reality that bad things happen. Now I do more than honour my sanity. I respect it. But there's one last thing I must do before I can sleep through the night and awake happy, with no sense of loss. Mr Pooch isn't going to like it.

I play with my Coco Pops for a while, using my spoon to sink the few that remain bobbing in the muddy milk, trying to summon the courage to say what needs to be said.

'What?' says Mr Pooch, patently bored by my cowardice.

'I need to tell you something,' I say, looking him in the eye. 'I must confront Him.'

Mr Pooch shakes his ugly little head.

'I have to tell Him I've won.'

'No. The dark holds a power over you. It's too dangerous. If you succumb...'

I nod. There's no need for him to finish the sentence. I'm prone to doing terrible things at night, after which I talk a load of drivel about Him making me do it. The fact that it's the truth is unimportant. I've still done what I've done. What I seem unable to explain to Mr Pooch is that if I don't risk facing Him, I'll never know if I can leave the night behind forever.

'He has to know I'm leaving,' I say. 'I have to be sure I've won.'

'Tomorrow is too important.'

'Gwendolyn thinks I'm ready.'

'Gwendolyn is a big fat bitch.'

'Coat it in sugar, Mr Pooch,' I mutter.

'All she cares about is her performance record and her bonus. She doesn't give a flying fornication about you.'

I can't argue – I know he's right.

'Do you trust me?' I ask.

'Do you trust yourself?' he counters.

There's a question. I feel a tear well in my eye, for Mr Pooch is as wise as Gandhi. Do I? Can I trust myself in the shadows? I wish I could say yes. Although a long absent feeling of hope has grown within me over the last few months, I cannot say for sure.

As if reading my thoughts, Mr Pooch says, 'You're strong, Brian, and I'm proud of your progress, but you can't risk seeing Him.'

*

We spend the day watching *Only Fools and Horses* repeats on Gold while grazing on junk food. Del Boy and Rodney are another positive part of my routine. They give me a sense of calm and I find I can watch every episode time and again without feeling like I'm wasting my life.

But as the day fades to dusk, I realise with certainty that I have to face Him. Hoping I can do this isn't enough. To cope with tomorrow's review, I have to be certain. I know Mr Pooch is looking out for me, but my gut tells me this is one of those rare occasions when he's wrong. I have to risk the worst to achieve my goal.

Throughout the day, I've made sure I keep waking Mr Pooch from his snoozing. If I keep disturbing him, he's more likely to sleep into the dark hours. He's vigilant, but he's old.

We come to the end of the episode about Peckham Spring Water. I go to make a cuppa, but there's no milk left. Good, perfect.

'We're out of milk,' I whisper. 'Just popping to the shop.' I unlock the backdoor and ooze into the night.

Part Two – The Bull

It's dark in the underpass and I've acquired milk. I managed to make the purchase without maiming anybody, so I'm feeling particularly pleased with myself. I can do this.

I've chosen this part of the city for a reason. Crime rates are high. I'm more likely to be confronted by an opportunity to face Him while only endangering those who deserve punishment.

The deeper into the shadows I move, the more I become aware of the cravings. *Fags, whiskey, sharp metal, soft flesh.* Recognising the negative thought pattern, I concentrate on my purpose, just like Mr Pooch taught me. *Buy milk, walk home, don't kill anyone.*

I'm concentrating so hard that I almost fail to notice three figures emerging from the shadows. Two of them carry knives, the other a bad case of acne and cruel eyes.

So here it is, a chance to say goodbye to the night, an opportunity to bid farewell to Him. I say, 'Smoo Choo is a Magic Moo, who keeps the land safe from harm. He lives in the Devonshire countryside, in a cowshed on Milky Moo Farm.'

And then he's there, a massive bull that walks like a

biped and wears a tattered cape. His horns glisten like poisoned blades of silver. Smoke curls from his nostrils, between which dangles a nose-ring of flaming metal.

The three figures start sniggering, blissfully unaware of the danger they're in. All they hear is a children's rhyme on the lips of a lunatic. They can't see what I see.

'It's been a long time, Brian,' says Smoo Choo, his voice as empty as death. 'I imagine you're gagging to release some kill-crazy-woo-ha?' I remember when the sound of that voice would fill me with peace, for it rang with the confidence of a decision maker – someone who could guide me. That was a long time ago. Now I hear it for the poison it is.

'No,' I say, watching the three figures advance, obviously bemused by my lack of fear and the fact I'm talking to empty space. 'I'm here to say goodbye.'

'You think yourself strong enough?'

'I do, Magic Moo.'

Smoo Choo smiles thinly. 'How foolish.'

'Who you talking to?' asks Spotty. The three youths spread out to surround me.

'Smoo Choo,' I reply, nodding at the mammoth bull they're blind to.

Spotty nods like a ham actor, as if he can see what I see. 'Who's he then?'

'An enchanted bull who walks like a man.'

I can see the conviction in my statement confusing them. The two knife boys laugh nervously. Spotty smirks. I know from experience that if you show no fear to pricks with knives, they don't really know what to do with it.

'Look, retard,' says Spotty, 'tell your mate with the udders to piss off.' His friends undertake some orchestrated sniggering. 'Then hand over your wallet.'

I notice Smoo Choo watching me with interest. It's as if he can sense that I want to lash out and is amused by the fight I'm putting up. He thinks I'll fail. He believes he's won.

'Look, we don't want to hurt you,' says Spotty, his eyes telling a different story. 'Tell Mr Choo his uncle Bo said it was OK for us to take your money. You know his uncle, don't you? Bo Vine?'

This resulted in some genuine laughter and finger pointing. Fair do's. Clever idea, but I find Spotty's laughter hard to bear. His manner is cruel and the pointing, well, that's just rude. For the first time I feel I may lose the fight.

'This imbecile dares to mock me?' Smoo Choo's voice rumbles like thunder. He's ignoring me now, his livid eyes focussed on Spotty. 'You mean to let them insult me like this and do nothing?' I look up and see Smoo Choo's cape ignite, becoming a sweeping mass of red flame. Now he's 10, 11, 12 feet tall, his face a mass of scowling wrinkles, his eyes as black as tar. 'Kill them,' he bellows.

'You do it,' I say. He turns towards me, malice dancing in his eyes. 'Can't, can you?'

'Do as I decree.'

I shake my head and recite the words I've never dared to before. 'Smoo Choo's tired, the day is saved, all is peaceful and calm. So he lays himself down to sleep in the hay, in his cowshed on Milky Moo Farm.'

A look of disbelief washes over Smoo Choo's face. I see his fury turn to fear. Then, he's gone.

I fall under an onslaught of punches. The three thugs have gathered the courage to launch themselves at me. As I fall, they kick and stab. I do nothing but smile. Their faces are alive with victory. They'll find 20 quid in my wallet. It's a lot of money to me, but let them take it. It's a cheap price to pay for the fight I've just won.

Now I know. Now I'm sure.

Part Three – The Madman

I wake in a hospital bed. Apparently I'm lucky to be alive. The police ask me some questions and I identify Spotty from a photo which seems to please them. A month later I'm discharged and return home.

I get out of the taxi, enter the house, and at last it sinks in: The battle is over. An incredible sense of relief consumes me. I stagger to the couch and sit trembling, relishing the quiet of an empty space after the hubbub of hospital.

Mr Pooch stalks into the room, looking properly pissed off. He hops onto the arm of the chair and stares at me. After a long silence, he says, 'Well?'

I tell him the story. His unblinking eyes stay locked to mine the entire time. I conclude with, '...and tomorrow, I have my review.'

'Gwendolyn visited you?'

'No. She called and asked one of the nurses to let me know.'

'Quelle surprise,' he mutters.

'Doesn't matter,' I say. 'I've won.'

'Not quite.'

'What do you mean?'

'You're having a conversation with a talking cat.'

'No, no, no—'

'You left the bull behind. You have to do the same to me.'

'I can't.'

'Turn off your doom siren. I'll still be here, I just won't be able to talk.'

'It won't be the same.'

'Do you want to say goodbye to the Madman?'

A tear wells in my eye. 'More than anything.'

'Then you have no choice.'

*

Gwendolyn arrives 35 minutes late and acts like she's early. She's lost some weight and her new tan suggests she's recently been in the close vicinity of a nuclear explosion. The stink of perfume fills the room as she sits at the kitchen table and prepares her papers.

'Be a love and make me some tea,' she says.

'White with two?' I ask.

'No sugar, Brian. The new me is sweet enough.'

I make us both a cuppa and join her at the table. Mr Pooch hops onto one of the empty chairs and stares at Gwendolyn. She seems blind to the hatred festering in his eyes and goes to pet him, making some inane 'cutesy wootsy' noises.

'So,' I say, drawing her attention before she can touch Mr Pooch and give him the opportunity to attack her. 'What happens today? I assumed there'd be someone with you.'

She gives me a patronising smile. 'No, Brian, today I make my decision. Then, if I'm happy, we go to the review board. If that happens, I'll tell you exactly what to say and when, so there's nothing to worry about. It'll be a doddle.'

It amazes me that she's failed to consider how unlike a doddle it might be for someone like me. From how many people has she withdrawn assistance, allowing them back onto the streets before they're ready? If Smoo Choo were still around, he'd probably make me stop her. I'm relieved to feel no arousal at the idea. No dark thoughts. Nothing, save disappointment at being let down by someone who is supposed to help me.

'So,' she says, taking a sip of her tea, 'as you know, there are stringent rules in place to make sure you're fully rehabilitated.' I nod. 'Have you been meditating?'

Yes, in my own special way, I suppose I have. I decide against voicing the thought. Instead I say, 'I've had an epiphany.'

'Really?' She sounds as interested as an atheist answering the door to a Jehovah's Witness. 'Tell me about it.'

'I... Sorry, this is very hard for me to explain.'

'Take all the time you need.'

'I feel different. I've been having inspiring thoughts, like there's... I don't know, a new me surfacing.' This is so hard. I'm aware I'm pausing for ages between words. I can see Gwendolyn's eyes glazing over, but this doesn't matter to me. She has no idea what I've done. I'd be in prison if they knew who I really was. I'm amazed they never worked it out. OK, Smoo Choo ensured I never left any evidence, but if all the cop shows on TV are to be believed, they should have caught me years ago. Eventually I was arrested for GBH and, due to my clean record and psychiatric history, they helped me readjust, ready to re-join society.

I realise that I'm trying to understand what's happened to me. I'm not hiding from the difficult questions I've avoided in the past. I look at Mr Pooch. His stare is absent of its usual contempt, replaced with anticipation, as though he's proud and willing me to go on.

'I'm considering positive ways forward,' I say. 'Things I can do to better myself, to help others, to try to make up for the bad things I've done. I've always had an overactive imagination, so I thought I might channel that creativity into something positive, maybe have a go at writing.'

'That's good, Brian,' says Gwendolyn, stifling a yawn. Her gaze moves back towards me from the fascinating vista of the breezeblock wall that can be viewed from my kitchen window. 'This just reinforces what I've believed all along. You're ready. I'll book a date with the review board and then we'll talk about what you need to say. Sound good?'

It sounds frightening, but I nod. I feel ready.

Gwendolyn fills out some paperwork, coerces me into signing it without reading it properly, and leaves.

I turn on the TV and sit in my armchair. I'm not trembling anymore. I feel calm. I pick up the children's book that rests on the table and think of my mother, how she would read me the stories of Smoo Choo the Magic Moo every night, no matter what my father had done to her. I remember when I first recited the opening words aloud, how He had come to me and showed me what I should do. I recall the knife, the blood, my father gurgling. The memory used to fill me with a sense of righteousness and glee. Now it just makes me sad.

Have I really succeeded? Has the will to heal mental scars done what medication couldn't? I know I've been determined, I've desired this more than life itself, but can you quit anything, be it nicotine, alcohol, narcotics or the lust for blood, just because you want to? And can you then channel all that misspent energy into something good? I don't know, but I intend to find out.

I look at the ugly little cat sitting opposite me. 'Have I done it?' I whisper. 'Have I really said goodbye to the Madman?'

'Meow,' says Mr Pooch.

~

MR KILL

1

Mrs Ida Wadworth is looking at me sceptically. I've explained that I can't resuscitate the dead worm she's produced from her pocket. She seems to be having trouble accepting my prognosis.

'But you're a vet,' she says.

'No I'm not.'

'It says so on your door.'

'No it doesn't.'

She surveys me with unmasked contempt. 'Are you going to save my worm?'

'It's been cut in half.'

'I know that, you fool. I did it with my trowel.'

'Even if I were a vet, there is no way to reanimate a decapitated worm.'

'So you *are* a vet.'

'No. I'm a doctor.'

Ida scrutinises me with rheumy eyes, her purple hair rinse glowing with alien phosphorescence. 'You look like a vet to me.'

I've run out of different ways to say the same thing. Thankfully, Ida moves towards the door. As she leaves, I receive a scowl 80 years in the making, but I discern a hint of disappointment in her glare, as though she had expected more from me. The door clicks shut behind her.

I sit for a minute and consider the patient I've just seen. Could she be a potential candidate for The Programme? No. She might be senile, but I enjoy Ida's visits. She isn't a bad person and, although rude, she often delivers the unexpected into an otherwise predictable day. With her walking its streets, the village of Dingle Green is a more interesting place to live.

As I turn back to my computer, I feel an intense pain in my head. It arrives from nowhere. I reach up to rub my scalp. As quickly as it materialised, the pain vanishes, as though it were never present. I investigate with my fingertips, half expecting to see blood, but there is nothing. Feeling slightly disorientated, I reach out and press the buzzer to summon my next patient. The room shifts slightly, taking on a hazy quality. I wipe my forehead, but my skin is dry.

Looking back at my computer screen, I see most of the details for my next patient are missing. I click refresh. Now there's even less information.

I jump with surprise as I notice a man in the room, sitting on the chair Ida vacated. He's watching me intently. I didn't hear him enter the room, or notice any movement. I feel myself redden as though caught in the middle of some nefarious act.

The man is dressed in black, his leather coat long and worn. He has mutton chops on his cheeks, but manages to wear them more like Wolverine than John McCririck. His hair is dark and streaked with grey. Pallid skin is clamped tightly to his skull, making him look ill. In contrast, his stare burns with life. I find it unnerving.

'I'm afraid we're having some computer problems,' I say. 'Can I take your name?'

'Kill.'

'I'm sorry?'

'Kill.' The man's eyes are a piercing grey, the colour of stormy sky.

'Mr Kill... OK. Forename?'

'Slash.'

Marvellous. A joker. Or a fruitcake. I hope he's the latter. It might mean he's eligible for The Programme.

'Middle names?'

'Hack, Maim.'

'You expect me to believe your name is Slash Hack Maim Kill?' I look up and wish I hadn't. Mr Kill's expression indicates two things. One: He is indeed Mr Slash Hack Maim Kill. Two: If he's asked his name again, I might come out of this encounter one testicle down. 'Your parents must have had a sense of humour.'

He smiles thinly. 'My old man likes Frank Zappa.'

Now my computer screen is completely blank. 'I'm sorry,' I say as I pick up the phone. 'Please bear with me.' The phone's dead, too, and I notice the second hand on my clock has stopped moving. Have we had a power cut?

'I hear things,' says Kill. I jump again, this time because his voice is so close. He's pulled his chair towards me, but I didn't see or hear a thing.

'Voices?'

'Kind of.'

'Do they tell you things?'

Kill leans forward, as though to impart a dreadful secret. 'The voices sing to me.'

I feel my neck tingle with gooseflesh and simultaneously fight the urge to laugh. A picture grows in my mind of the devil singing a lullaby to this man, tickling his chin lovingly with a black, pointed talon.

'The voices are accompanied by guitars, bass and drums,' Kill continues. 'Amazing riffs, rolling rhythms, thundering bass lines. But recently the music has changed.'

'How so?'

'The voices have started singing about you.'

There's something about the way he imparts this information that makes me feel my life expectancy has diminished. The urge to laugh deserts me. 'Me?'

'I know what you've done.'

Done? What have I done?

'You know,' he says.

Now I feel like I'm the patient and he's the doctor. I didn't say that out loud.

'No, you didn't. The voices that sing to me have become one – your voice. Lately it's been getting louder. Now it's so loud it's drowning out the rest of the band, and I'm a man who prefers instrumentals.'

I wonder if I'm dreaming. No, dreams hold a certain recognisable quality, something that tells you, deep down, that it's just a dream. This is happening. The question I can't answer is: *What* is happening?

I fight an unfamiliar feeling. It takes me a while to recognise it as panic. My eyes are drawn to Kill's face. Who is this man? He arrived like a ghost. And he says he hears voices. Is he toying with me? Usually, people who hear things have some sort of mannerism: a twitch or social inability. The chilling thing about Mr Kill is his lucidity. Then, realisation strikes.

'You're not real.'

'So why are you talking to me?'

I consider this. Maybe Kill is a figment of my imagination; I've been working a lot lately and feeling exhausted. I close my eyes for a few seconds and then open them. He's still there. I reach out and touch his arm. He feels solid, but there's something amiss. I turn his hand palm upwards and press my fingertips against his wrist bone, feeling for a palpitation of the radial artery.

'You have no pulse.'

He nods, as if I'm stating the obvious rather than understanding the entire situation. 'I don't need one.' His stare bores into me like two spinning drill bits. 'Neither do you.'

I grab my wrist. There's no pulse. 'I'm dead?'

'Yes. Your body is in your office. This is limbo, the place between life and death.'

I look around. 'We're in my office.'

'No. What we see around us is a reflection of the moment of your death. Look on it like a warehouse – a holding area for your spirit while I decide the manner of your deliverance.'

'Who the hell are you? Death?'

'No. I'm Kill. Death is my father. Death waits for those who've died. I wait for those who've been killed.'

'Killed...' He nods. 'I was murdered?'

'Yes.' His patience seems to be ebbing. Do I care? No. I'm dead. What can he do to hurt me now?

'You'd be surprised,' he says.

I don't like that he can read my thoughts. I'm finding the lack of privacy unsettling.

'Get used to it.'

I didn't know I was dead until Kill had spelled it out for me. How could someone kill me without me realising it?

'The killer was gifted. He planned and executed the murder perfectly.' He gives me the drill stare again. 'The problem with your Programme is you only considered the candidates and those they might harm. You failed to consider those who might be negatively affected by your actions. Remember your last kill?'

'Yes.' It had saddened me, but she had to be stopped. She couldn't accept living with HIV, couldn't forgive the man that had infected her. Being pretty, she used her looks to seduce men and spread the disease. For her, it represented revenge.

'Her father is a retired soldier,' said Kill. 'He saw you leaving the scene. He decided to deal with you himself. Remember the sudden pain you felt in your head?' I nod. 'It was a bullet.'

I rub the back of my head. I can feel no wound. But then, if Kill is to be believed, I am no longer in my body.

I feel confused. Cheated. It all seems so unfair. 'But my life's work isn't complete.'

'Neither were the participants' in your Programme. I'm familiar with your work. I've met all your victims.'

'Victims?' I spit the word. If he were truly familiar with The Programme, he'd realise there were no victims. More lives would be saved in the absence of the sadistic, selfish, twisted and cruel. And I always carefully consider each candidate, study them, making sure they're appropriate.

'True, but remember the banker?'

I look blankly at him. There have been so many...

'He liked to drink,' continues Kill. 'Killed a girl in a hit and run.'

I nod. 'He'd have done it again.'

'He did. You murdered his twin.'

Could I have made such an idiotic error? Surely not. I was meticulous. I always made sure.

'You tried, but everyone makes mistakes. Why did you think you wouldn't? Ironically, your arrogance would make you a candidate for your own Programme.' A thin smile touches Kill's lips. I don't like it. He's laughing at me, not with me.

'So,' I say, not hiding my irritation. 'What happens now?'

His smile fades. 'I shall ask you one simple question. Your answer will determine your path into the Ever.' He reaches inside his jacket and pulls out two sickles. One has a shimmering blade of sunlight, the other is the colour of night. They sizzle as he moves them through the air. 'Are you ready?'

For once I feel I know what's coming next and this fills me with calm. The confusion I have experienced until now washes away. Kill's manner has changed. He knows I know. I am dead. Eternity awaits. Have I done wrong? No. I have saved countless lives with no expectation of recognition for my achievements. Should I give an answer I believe he wants to hear? No. I can't. He'd know I lied. All I can do is answer honestly. I'm ready for judgement.

'Do you admit doing wrong?'

'No. I did no wrong.'

'I bid you farewell, Dr William Hatton.'

Kill swings the two sickles. They plunge into my chest. There is no pain. Kill is gone. My office is gone. Everything is gone.

2

I'm in the dark. Damp earth presses around me. The feeling is pleasant. I'm content in the cold, wriggling forward, eating that which is in front of me, leaving that which is behind me. I feel safe.

Everything around me erupts. Cold metal rips into my midriff. Soil tumbles. Light dazzles. I feel a warm hand on my cold body. I wriggle, finding the heat distressing. A pair of rheumy eyes peer at me, surrounded by a halo of purple.

'Oh dear,' says Ida Wadworth. 'Don't worry, little worm, I know where to take you. If there's one man who can save your soul, it's William Hatton.'

~

ALTERNATIVE AFTERLIVES

THE TREASURE NO THIEF CAN STEAL

1

Before me is a panoramic view. Usually, beautiful scenery makes me feel calm. Not today. I'm tied to a tree on snow-covered ground and my fingers are numb.

Over the past week I've been dragged up a mountain by my captor, his cruel eyes betraying a desire that he's unable to act on. He needs me as he believes me to be – untouched. I smile at the thought.

'What's funny, bitch?'

He wants me, but can't have me. He hates me, but needs me alive. At least I'm enjoying his frustration.

I stare at him, refusing to answer.

'Smile while you can, pretty one,' he says. 'What you got coming's gonna make a mess of your face.'

I'm trying to remain strong, but the callous way he speaks makes my impending death inescapable.

My captor chuckles.

Feeling tears on my cheek, I stare out over the vista before me.

We're on the higher slopes of Mount Holne, where the Gordesian Mountains divide to form the borders of Kort Eavenhow, Thirl Mere and Lostwithiel. If you use your imagination, the lay of the mountains to the northwest looks like the gargantuan maw of a slain creature. The view is known as The Jaws. This spectacle is said to have inspired a popular myth: The entire Gordesian mountain range was created by a dragon's fallen body. It fell in a fight with an unnamed god who, thirsty from battle, drank from the sea so deeply that the surrounding lands were revealed.

Sitting here, witnessing this spectacle for the first time, makes the legend seem plausible. There are worse places to die.

My captor moves to sit near me, seemingly disappointed by my regained composure. He eats some salted beef and slurps water. I watch him, unable to take my eyes from the food.

When he's done eating, he feeds me the few remaining scraps. I gobble them, too hungry to decline.

He watches me, cocking his head with interest. My eyes mist and I realise I'm hallucinating. He looks like a plucked chicken, basted and stuffed, ready to cook, but his eyes are alive, observing me as though I'm the meal ready for the oven. I wonder what narcotic he's fed me.

'Night, night,' he says. 'You're gonna wake up dead, pretty bitch.' His voice sounds distant. My consciousness fades.

2

My head feels like it's been used as an anvil. I groan and roll onto my side, forcing my eyes open.

The first thing I see is the box. It sits upon a plinth in a shaft of sunlight, beautifully crafted from wood and inlaid with ivory. It might be a trick of the light, or the residue of narcotics in my system, but it looks like a hazy aura is emanating from the object, giving it an auburn glow. Transfixed, I stand and approach on trembling legs.

Up close, the workmanship looks even more impressive, every joint invisible. Studying the ivory inlay more carefully, I see an ornate, cobweb-like pattern. As I examine it, I realise that words are hidden within the design:

Trickery, trappery, feeding the need,
Meat for the beast, drawn by rumour and greed.

As I reach forward, a guttural growl echoes in the darkness. My senses return and I'm suddenly aware of my surroundings.

I'm in the centre of a large cavern, which is illuminated by a pillar of sunlight, radiating from a crevice high in the rooftop. The cave stinks of death. Skulls litter the floor.

Mountains of bones are piled against one wall, surrounded by a horde of interesting items: swords, parchments, armour and archaic contraptions.

I realise where I must be. The heap of bones corresponds with stories of Grimdune, a bestial collector of artefacts and relics. Until now, I'd assumed the tales to be myth.

'What possessed you to bring me here?' I whisper to my absent captor.

'Greed.'

The voice that answers me is deep and resonant. Something vast moves in the cavern's shadows. I see two huge eyeballs glint on the edge of the shaft of sunlight. As the creature moves closer, its pupils shrink from distended yellow circles to putrid slits, surrounded by black, rust-flecked irises.

A gigantic head appears from the shadows, followed

by a long neck and immense shoulders. It's a dragon, but like none I've ever seen depicted in books. It's covered in scales that are the grey of death and interlinked like armour. They rasp against each other as it moves, while its eyes gleam with cunning.

I feel an impossible chill exuding from the creature's body, so intense it burns. Black fog pours from its nostrils towards the floor, where the vapour gropes around, like a living mist in search of souls.

This must be Grimdune.

He eyes me like a cat observing a vole beneath its paw. The corners of his mouth twitch, as if trying to understand a smile for the first time. I feel like he's toying with me, hoping fear might tenderise my flesh before he eats. This angers me. My legs cease to tremble and I find my voice.

'Why haven't you eaten me?'

'Why do you think?' As he speaks, the dragon's dry lips move in front of jagged incisors, each of which is bigger than me.

'Because I'm not pure.'

Black fire erupts from the flared nostrils on Grimdune's snout as he snorts laughter. 'Tell me,' he says, 'can you detect the sexual exploits of a cow by eating steak?'

I feel stupid. 'Why then?'

'I'm intrigued to know what you're basted in before I bite.'

I look down. I'm naked and covered in filth. Goo glistens on my skin. Dirt and dust have stuck to the translucent residue, clothing me in grime. I rub at the gloop and find it's sticky and smells sweet.

Looking up, I see Grimdune studying my expression closely. 'Where are you?' he asks, looking through me, addressing someone else. 'I can smell you. Your gluttony. Your cowardice. Show yourself.'

My captor emerges from the shadows of a crack in the cave wall, proffering something in his right hand as if it will protect him.

'Falcon,' Grimdune rasps. 'I heard you were dead.'

I'm shocked to hear the name. The Falcon has a reputation as a master of thievery and a roguish womaniser. Could the man that kidnapped me really be a thief of such renown?

He moves closer to the dragon. Clasped between his thumb and forefinger, I see a pointed tooth.

'It helps a thief when he's thought dead,' Falcon says.

Grimdune tilts his head slightly, observing the trinket Falcon proffers. 'What is it you think you have?'

'Plan B. It's the last tooth of the vampires of the Deep Dream Peaks. They cursed you, but we hunted them, killed them. This thing here's the last bit of them, the only piece not burned or crushed. It keeps you alive.'

'I am undead. I have no life to empower.'

I see Falcon's confidence wavering. 'Give me the box, lizard.'

'You meant to thwart me by covering a whore in poison and now you're threatening me with a vampire's tooth while voicing petty insults? I would expect more from a man of your reputation. Tell me. The day your parents passed, did you die too?'

'What?'

'If you break my mother's tooth, why should I perish?'

Falcon shakes his head. 'This ain't your mother's tooth. Give me what I want.'

'And what's that?'

'The box. What's in it. To live forever.' He sounds flustered. 'The magic that's in the damned box.'

'Immortals possess life everlasting, but they're as fragile as any living thing. Have you fully considered what you ask for? Immortality brings madness, for nothing can survive eternity.'

'Shut up your trickery.' Falcon is shouting now. 'Give me what I want.'

Grimdune moves his head back. The mist on his breath thickens, becoming an acrid smoke that belches from his mouth.

Falcon drops the tooth on the floor and moves his foot, ready to crush it. 'Do what I say.'

Grimdune spits a plume of black flame towards the cavern's roof. 'Neigen, Ert dwaller,' he bellows. 'Neigen.'

Although the language isn't familiar to me, Grimdune's meaning is obvious. Falcon stamps down hard on the tooth. I hear it crack. He grinds it into the cave floor beneath his boot and looks up expectantly. Hope fades from his face.

Grimdune is rising on monstrous hind legs, his wings spread to their full extent, the grey membrane stretching between the wing phalanges until it looks almost translucent. They are like the enormous wings of a bat, the patagium torn in places. His head moves up into the shaft of sunlight and I see his huge incisors gradually extend to monstrous proportions, ripping from the grey gums in his upper jaw. Black venom exudes from within the enamel, trickling down the fangs to form poisonous drips that fall from the tooth tips and meet the stone floor of the cave with a hiss.

'Didn't think to coat yourself in poison, did you?'

says Grimdune.

Falcon turns to run, but the dragon lunges. His jaws snap shut. Falcon is gone.

The dragon hunkers down guardedly, like a predator protecting its kill, enveloped by its wings. There's a disgusting sucking noise. Then the wings fold back and he turns towards me. On the floor, where Falcon had stood, a fresh, gleaming skull has joined the masses.

I watch the dragon for a moment, then say, 'The box is empty, isn't it?'

'As empty as avarice allows.' The dragon moves closer, his eyes playful.

'You can't eat me,' I say.

'But I can kill you.'

I drop to one knee and bow my head. I've heard that dragon's respond well to subservience and I'm damned if I'm just going to stand there and wait to die. I have to try. 'My name is Lila. I was kidnapped and brought here against my will as a sacrifice. My captor is gone. My life is yours. I beg you to spare me.'

I feel the cold of Grimdune against my skin. I look up and find his head close. 'Give me good reason.'

'I can tell of what I've seen here today. I'm pretty. Men will listen.'

'What benefit is that to me?'

'It proves the box exists, it confirms the legends.'

'And then more will come, won't they, Lila?'

Grimdune withdraws into the shadows until I can see only one great eyeball staring at me. 'I appreciate guile. You'll find candles beneath a ledge at the back of the cavern, along with furs and a pool of water. It's clean enough to drink. Follow the tunnels marked with an insignia of the sun. Go.'

3

As I walk from the cavern, wrapped in warm clothing, holding a flickering candle, I realise that the ornate box in Grimdune's lair will never be empty. It will always be filled with dreams and intrigue. Even I feel an urge to go back and open it, to see if I'm right – to see if it's empty. But Falcon's death is too fresh in my mind. I'm alive and I want to stay that way.

A strange thought manifests in my mind – I hope the memory of Falcon's death stays with me forever. I never want to return here, seeking the treasure no thief can steal.

~

ALTERNATIVE AFTERLIVES

SHOT IN THE HEAD AND LEFT FOR DEAD

1

I'm sweating, captivated by the frenzy of a beat so powerful it sounds like a living, breathing monster. The rhythm section motor behind me like a hell-fuelled engine. Smoke clouds the air and the stage lights burn.

As Ian Maiden's bass rumbles with wrath, Jack Sabbath unleashes a demonic riff, accompanying the thundering rhythm. The atmosphere is vibrant, the crowd are hungry and Wembley Stadium throbs with life. The stage shakes beneath my feet with the thrum of the music and the mass of bodies before me, all bouncing in unison.

Dwight Snake moves to the front of the stage. He points back at me and shouts, 'You wanna hear some guitar, London?' The crowd roar. 'You asked for it, you metal maniacs. I give you, Dave,

'Against,

'The,

'Machiiiiiiine.'

I face my wall of Marshalls and allow the hum of feedback to grow. The volume becomes painful before I turn to face the audience, unleashing a solo that feels as though it's oozing from my fingertips rather than me having to play it. As I hold the final note and push down hard on my Les Paul's whammy bar, Dwight begins to holler his lyrics.

'Going down the road and what did I see?'

The 100,000 strong crowd are singing with him, almost drowning him out.

'6,000 psychos, coming at me.'

Maiden and I move in front of the drum kit, and watch the blur of sticks and the spray of sweat as Geoff Leppard hammers out the rhythm.

'I ran, I ran, I fuckin' ran.'

We strike a chord hard, letting the sound resonate while the drums stop dead.

'But I wasn't fast enough,' growls Dwight.

Sabbath, Maiden and I approach our mikes for the chorus as the drums explode back into life, accompanied by pyrotechnics blasting flames into the air from either side of the stage.

'Shot in the head,' Dwight hollers.

'And left for dead,' we reply.

'Shot in the head.' Dwight cups his left hand around his ear and holds his mike towards the audience.

'And left for dead,' they chant.

'Shot in the head.'

'And left for dead.'

'I was shot in the head.' Dwight makes a sweeping slash through the air with his right hand and the music stops instantly, save for the soft count of Leppard's hi-hat, keeping the beat. 'And left for...' The noise of the crowd begins to grow, but before it can crescendo, the music crashes back in and Dwight screams, 'Deeeeeeeeeeeeeeeeeead.'

I'm about to dive down the fretboard out of a high lick and join Jack Sabbath with the main riff when I see a bright flash from somewhere near the front of the crowd. It stands out amongst multiple camera flashes and the glow of mobile phones. It's crisp and definite, filled with purpose and pain.

Something smashes into my face. Everything changes.

2

I'm lying on the stage, but it's empty. Everything looks grey. There's no band, no gear, no pyrotechnics and no crowd. After all the mayhem, the colourless silence seems surreal.

Above me, one solitary spotlight shines a cold circle of illumination, like a grey moon. The light looks inviting and I wonder what it might be like to drift towards it, curl up and sleep.

'Oh no you don't, you lazy git.'

A figure moves out of the shadows. At first, the way the person moves makes me think it might be my dad. As they step into the light, I realise it's me. A much older me, but definitely me. The tattoo on my forearm is faded, but still spelt wrong. Amidst the skulls, flames and motorcycles, a banner reads 'Rock 'n' Role'. You've got to be pretty poor at spelling to get that wrong. Or paralytic on Natch. Unfortunately, the tattooist was the former and I was the latter.

'Nice mullet,' I say, getting to my feet.

'It's on your head, asshole,' Old Dave replies.

Age doesn't seem to have tamed my language. 'Am I dead?' I ask.

'Nope, not yet.'

'So what's going on?'

Old Dave grins, 'Man, this is going to fuck your

mind.'

Given the current situation, I sense wisdom in Old Dave's words. Feeling something trickle down my face, I wipe it away. Inspecting my fingers, I see blood. It looks unnaturally red amidst the grey pallor of everything else.

'You've been shot in the head,' says Old Dave.

'And left for dead,' I say.

'Not quite. I'm here.'

'But you're me. Does that count?'

'I told you this would fuck your mind.' Old Dave grins, revealing too few teeth for my liking, which reminds me that I need to sort out a dental appointment.

'My brain hurts,' I mumble.

'OK, let's get all the mind-blowing shit done in one hit. I'm dead. I... *we* got shot by some moron who did too many drugs and thought Dwight's lyrics were some sort of divine fuckin' message.'

'To shoot me?'

'LSD doesn't induce rationality.' Old Dave gives me a wink which makes him look just like Dad. 'When this happened to me, there was no one here. I saw that light,' he says, pointing at the grey-moon-spotlight-thing, 'and I drifted towards it. Now I'm some sort of ghost that gets older, has a mullet and all my fuckin' teeth are falling out. I'm seriously hoping I'm not immortal, because ghosts feel all sorts, including pain.'

'But you're me and I'm you. So this happened to you, too. You can't be dead.'

'Wrong. You have to go through the cycle once, or I wouldn't be able to be here imparting all my 'been there, done that, it's a shit idea, don't do it' wisdom, would I? We're both Dave Against The Machine, but now this has happened, we're on different paths.'

'So we're different people?'

'Yes, and no, but yes makes things easier to get your head around.'

My head isn't getting around anything, least of all having a bullet lodged in it. This must be a dream, or a hallucination. Dwight did say he had some new pills he wanted us to try. Maybe he spiked our drinks.

As if reading my mind, Old Dave slaps me in the face, hard.

'This is real?' I ask.

He grins. 'Realer than tax. You with me so far?'

'You're dead. I'm not... yet. We're both Dave, the same Dave, but you're you and I'm me. That the basic gist?'

'You're on fire.'

'Is that all the mind-blowing shit done with?'

'Oh no,' chuckles Old Dave, 'there's a whole dimension of crazy for you to wade your stumpy little legs through yet.'

'One hit, you said.'

'Stop interrupting, then.'

I give him a nod, and gesture for him to continue using my middle finger.

'I want you to live,' says Old Dave. 'Trust me, being a ghost is a pile of shite. You don't wanna do it. But more important, back in the land of the living, the world has gone bat-shit mental. Not long after we were shot, and I'm talking moments, all the active volcanos erupted.'

'What? All of them?'

'Yeah.'

'How many?'

'About 1,500.'

'There's that many?'

Old Dave gives me a look I have yet to hone. It simply suggests that the wisest decision for on-going lifelong happiness would be to stop talking. I shut up, making a mental note to work on that look. It's awesome.

'Out of the volcanos came an infection that spread like buggery,' he continues, 'instantly turning about half the human race into zombies.'

'You're shitting me.'

'Nope. And there's more. With the lava came monsters. Big fuckin' things. Mean enough to make Andy McNab cack his pants.'

'So the world's a volcano-ridden mess,' I say, 'with zombies and lava-monsters running around killing everyone?' Sounds kind of cool, but not somewhere you'd want to live. Like Belgium.

'Oh no. These monsters, they might be all lava and claws and breath like sulphur, but they ain't stupid. They've got a taste for zombies, so it's in their interest to farm them, see? Make sure their food don't run out.'

'No way.'

'Yes way. And what do zombies like to eat?'

'Brains.'

'Boom. But zombies don't breed, do they? They turn humans into zombies. So now there's these big-ass farms to grow food for humans. Then they farm the humans to become infected by zombies so there's enough zombies for all the monsters to eat.'

Volcanoes, zombies and monsters, resulting in a food chain nightmare. It's too much to take in. 'Please tell me that's it,' I say.

'Almost,' says Old Dave. He takes a meaningful pause, then says, 'You can stop it.'

This is now officially mental. The premise sounds like

it might make a great B-Movie, if you could find an investor with pots of money and a low IQ, but not something that's actually happening. No way.

'This is a wind up,' I say.

'No, it's not.'

'How do you know all this?'

'The story's long, boring and hard to believe. Let's just say there's some knowledgeable beings this side of life, and I work for one of them.'

'I don't buy it.'

'You're half past dead, talking to yourself – an older you that's a ghost. Open your mind, asshole.'

He has a point. 'OK, you gonna tell me how I stop it all?'

'You can't stop it. It's happening no matter what you do.'

'You just said I could.'

'OK, 'stop' was a bit misleading. The zombies and the monsters, that's happening. All the ape-shit farming – *that* you can do something about. In this soon to be reality nightmare, we've moved down to third on the food chain, right?'

'And we need to be back to number one,' I say.

'No. You need to move us down to fourth.'

'What? How?'

'By summoning something that's bigger and badder than the monsters and zombies combined. Something with a taste for lava-monsters that finds humans good company.'

I go to speak, but Old Dave interrupts me. 'We ain't got much time. If you're going back, you need to go soon or you'll die. So listen.' I nod. 'There's a song brewing and the band has been jamming it, saving it for the right moment. I know it, because I was jamming it before I decided to be a lazy git and take the easy-way-out-and-go-to-sleep-in-the-pretty-fuckin'-light   ponce's road to ghostdom.'

He's right. We have got a song brewing, and it's a beauty. 'And?'

'You got to play it, and play it loud.'

'That's it?'

'Not quite.'

Old Dave reaches out and grabs either side of my head in his hands. Hideous visions fill my mind, of the most bizarre farming practices imaginable. You thought farmers feeding cows to cows and BSE was bad? That was a meat production paradise in comparison to what I'm seeing.

'You're going back now, Dave.' Old Dave's voice echoes like the wind. 'Keep these images fresh in your mind. Use them as inspiration. Make the music happen. There's magic in that song. Don't think, just play. And play it fast.'

3

Sitting up, I feel the stage shake beneath me. The vibrations aren't coming from the thunder of music or the energy of the crowd – this feels like an earthquake. After the greyness of death, the noise and colour of life startle me, but not as much as what I see kicking off before me.

The audience is in pandemonium. Half of the crowd is trying to eat the other half's brains. Those who are reluctant to have their heads ripped open are trying to run away and/or kill their attackers with anything they can use as a weapon, including bits of other people.

Things couldn't be redder; it's like a tomato puree production factory.

Before I can fully digest the scene, a mass of smoking devilry dives out of the sky and starts munching zombies like a ravenous bulldozer. It's about the size of a three-bed semi. Its teeth are as big as buses and it stinks of volcano.

Ignoring the ache in my head, I wipe the blood out of my eyes and stand up. My head is pounding with pain and I want to puke. Adrenaline is all that's allowing me to function.

I look at the rest of the band. None of them seem to be zombies, although it's always hard to tell with the rhythm section. At the side of the stage I notice two of the roadies eating one of the sound guys, while my guitar tech is using a spare Les Paul to try to behead what used to be our A&R man.

I grab Maiden's arm. 'Fuck the fuck,' he says. 'What the bastard?' Eloquently put. Kind of sums up what I was thinking.

'Noise,' I scream. 'We need to make lots of it.'

He looks at me like I'm mad. Maybe I am. Bollocks to it. This zombie-monster-fest is coming to an end. Now.

I start up the riff to 'There's Something in my Pants and it's Evil'. The three-bed-semi-smoking-hell-monster screams and launches back into the air, out of Wembley's open roof, disappearing over the city of London.

Seeing the zombies all clasp their hands over their ears, Jack Sabbath joins me in the riff and Geoff Leppard hammers out a long, triplet-rich fill before settling into the rhythm. Dwight Snake looses a chaotic scream. Maiden slides into the bass riff, feeding the maelstrom.

Building the crescendo with a Hendrix-esque

improvised solo, I feel the magic of the band gestating. The pain from the bullet in my brain is forgotten.

'Fear, of the dark,' hollers Dwight.

As the music swells with life, a tear opens in the sky.

'Fires, the spark.'

Wreathed in flame, something humongous bursts through the portal in the sky.

'Sets my stomach shaking, my inner tubes are quaking, God only knows what my intestines are making.'

Something drops from my head. I look down and see a bullet. I quickly rub my forehead. The wound is gone. Old Dave was right – there is magic in the music.

'I got so scared I drank too much beer, my mud-flaps can't contain the smell of fear.'

The thing in the sky is immense. It must be miles long and looks like it's made out of molten metal. Explosions of fire erupt from its sides, seemingly guiding its flight. A mouth opens at the front of the thing, revealing a black void of death.

'There's something in my pants and it's evil.'

Never have lyrics been so poignant.

'Winking sphincter, the eye of a needle.' Dwight is howling the words like a madman, tearing his vocal chords to shreds. 'Badgers nose, it smells medieval.'

The thing we've summoned is gorging on the smoking-lava-hades-monsters. I notice hundreds of eyes shrouding the gargantuan mouth, glowing with dark intelligence. At first, I thought it was some kind of spaceship. Now, I realise it's alive.

'Ride the chocolate speedway just like Evel Knievel.'

As the massive thing comes nearer, zombies start exploding. Humans are being showered in tomatoey gore. Judging by the jubilant looks on their faces, this is better than being eaten.

With a titanic blast of its engines, the thing in the sky moves towards Wembley. Dwarfing the stadium, it hovers above us.

'My bitches, you've freed me,' it says, in a voice more formidable than death. 'I am the Molten Metal Death Machine.'

Sweet insanity, what next?

As if reading my mind, the Death Machine says, 'Now, we fly.'

Reality wobbles. Suddenly, we're on the Death Machine's back with all our instruments and amplification.

'Play,' it says. 'Play loud, my bitches. Let us purge your planet of filth and bring wrath to the skies.'

As we launch into the second verse of 'There's Something in my Pants and it's Evil', the Molten Metal Death Machine flies, pulsing our music out over London in waves of chaos. Everywhere we look, zombies and monsters explode like pots of Bolognese sauce in a microwave. Blood is spurting in torrents. The scene looks like the world's worst tomato ketchup advert.

4

'Cut,' shouts the director, Dan Halen.

I watch him turn to the producer, Tracy Dee Cee, who says, 'Heinz are going to love this. So are cinema audiences. Best ad we've ever made.'

'What about the rest of the population?' asks Halen. 'The storyline's implausible, the gore gratuitous. They'll hear about it, even if it is only shown before horror films.'

'It's going to upset people,' says Dee Cee. 'It's going to make them complain. And complaints mean publicity.'

'Could be bad publicity.'

'No such thing.'

'Can we go now?' I ask.

Halen waves his hand dismissively, without looking at us. I assume this means 'yes'.

'Condescending prick,' mutters Maiden, as we wander back to our dressing room.

'You reckon the fans will think we've sold out?' I ask 'You know, doing a ketchup advert. Not very rock 'n' roll, is it?'

Maiden shrugs. 'We got to eat.'

He's right. It's a problem for another day. Right now, I need to get out of my spandex. It's making my balls itch.

~

ALTERNATIVE AFTERLIVES

DIRTY DEEDS, DONE DIRT CHEAP

1

Charles Earnest Dorne looked at his watch. Twenty-one minutes had passed.

'Late,' he muttered.

He paced right, then left, and looked at his watch again. Twenty-two minutes.

'Unacceptable.'

He paced some more. Twenty-two and a half minutes.

'Intolerable.'

Aware of the frown creasing his face, Dorne paused, straightened his back and tried to clear his thoughts. When he was irritated, he became abrasive, more likely to make mistakes. This was going to be the most important meeting of his life. He had to focus.

Sucking in a breath, Dorne counted to 10, exhaled slowly and looked out of the window, seeking calm.

The view from the office block wasn't soothing. Tall glass buildings erupted from fog, like the masts of alien ships. One of them burned. Smoke gently swirled from the tower's exotic roof garden. Against the calm blue sky, this was the only indicator of the riots that raged beneath the mist.

As an umbrella in the roof-garden of the smoking tower burst into flame, Dorne tried to look away, but couldn't. His neglect had led to this. His incompetence. He had to watch.

A figure leapt from the rooftop. From this distance they seemed small, insignificant, unreal. As they fell, flames danced behind them, reflected in the glass exteriors of the surrounding office towers. Silently, the leaper was swallowed by the fog.

Slumping into a chair, Dorne closed his eyes, trying to focus on why he was here. But all he could see was the leaper, screaming soundlessly, their despair contagious.

2

Dorne had been waiting for over an hour. It had given him time to regain his composure and focus on what he must do. If the stories of the 4D 1C Shipping Company were true, all this could be fixed – *would* be fixed. Dorne had to ensure it.

He was in a large room that felt cramped, due to the amount of furniture it contained. Dorne disliked clutter, but there was a tantalising quality to his surroundings. An archaic desk. A Victorian leather chair. Shelves overloaded with books, scrolls and seafaring memorabilia. Dorne felt like he was in a museum. A shrine to simpler, more interesting times. Times of discovery.

Housed in a modern building, the room was an unexpected pleasure. As the grandfather clock in the corner ticked steadily, Dorne looked through the books. One stood out: *The Sea Beard Chronicles*. The spine was made from thick leather, beautifully carved and painted to resemble a swelling ocean. Dorne took it from the shelf and saw a boat on the cover. A pirate stood on the prow, clutching a melting clock.

Intrigued, Dorne leafed through the book and became absorbed in the tales of Sea Beard, a mythical pirate who could walk through time.

The more he read, the more the rumours that had brought him to this place seemed plausible. Slowly, his despair was replaced by hope.

3

A man entered the room before Dorne could finish Sea Beard's story. He was tall, but stooped, and powerfully built. Thick, greying hair was combed back from his face and tattoos decorated his forearms.

Ignoring Dorne, he took residence in the Victorian chair behind the ancient desk and started sorting through papers. Without looking up, he said, 'Sorry to keep you waiting, guv. Please, take a seat.'

'I already have.'

Dorne's tone was indignant. The man looked up. He regarded Dorne with eyes that glittered with colour; one was blue, the other tawny, flecked with gold.

'Can I get you a cuppa?' he asked.

'No.'

'Coffee then?'

'I'm not thirsty.'

The man turned and rummaged in a cupboard behind the desk. Eventually, he emerged holding a dusty bottle. 'Rum.'

'No, thank you.'

'That wasn't a question, guv.' He took two grimy

glasses from a drawer in his desk, filled them with dark liquid and placed one in front of Dorne.

'I'd prefer we get straight to business.'

'OK. Business it is.' The man folded his tattooed arms. One forearm was decorated with an elaborate anchor, surrounded by demonic mermaids, the other with a ship caught between the huge waves of a storm. 'What do you want?'

'My name is Charles Earnest Dorne. I'm the—'

'I know who you are, guv.'

'You must be Wilson.'

'I am. Two-Eyed Wilson, owner of 4D 1C Shipping.'

'Why 'Two-Eyed'?'

'Because I got two eyes.'

Dorne felt he was being tested. He softened his expression. 'I'm sorry. With all that's going on out there...' He glanced at the window. 'It's taking its toll on me. I apologise for being discourteous. I appreciate your hospitality, and your time.' Dorne picked up the glass Wilson had placed before him, inspected the contents, and then drank it in one gulp.

The liquid was foul. It tasted bitter and sweet at the same time. Dorne gagged.

Wilson smiled. 'Good, ain't it?'

'Delicious.'

Wilson downed his own drink, then poured them both more. 'So, what is it you want?'

'Someone killed.'

Wilson sat back in his chair and laughed.

'Did I say something funny?' Dorne asked.

'Politicians rarely say what they mean. It's refreshing to hear, is all.'

Dorne nodded.

'Who needs murdering?' Wilson asked.

'Me.'

This time Wilson didn't laugh. 'An expensive way to commit suicide, guv.'

'I need myself killed in the past.'

All signs of friendliness fell away from Wilson's face. 'I know I'm notorious as an undertaker of dirty deeds. And I'll admit, off the record of course, that I done plenty of them. But I ain't Dr Who.' Wilson stood up. 'I think you should leave.'

Dorne remained seated. 'I made a decision 11 years ago. A poor decision. It led to this.' He pointed at the window. 'It needs undoing.' He lifted the book he'd been reading. 'I understand Sea Beard can walk the paths of time.'

'Mythical characters often do magical things. That don't make it real.'

'Blake Fenton assured me that I could rely on your company's services.'

'Really? How is the old sod?'

'She still refuses to die, despite the tumour.'

'Fenton has little patience for politics. I'm surprised she tolerates you, guv.'

'She was a close friend of my mother. They schooled together. I think I am afforded more leeway than most. That said, when I last saw Aunt Blake, she told me I was becoming too conscientious. "Compassion is poisonous, darling," she said. "It makes one weak." She thinks I am no longer fit to lead.'

'Is she right?'

'Always.'

Wilson proffered his glass and said, 'To Fenton, dealer of harsh truths.'

Dorne raised his glass. They drank.

'Tell me more,' Wilson said, retaking his seat and

pouring fresh rum.

Dorne stood and looked out of the window. More people were hurling themselves from the burning tower opposite.

'The malcontent, the riots, the threat to the establishment.' Dorne could hear the waver of guilt in his own voice. 'The suffering. All this, it's my doing. My fault. The consequence of one poor decision. I placed my trust in the powerful and failed the poor.' He turned to face Wilson. 'I've taken counsel from my cabinet, advisors, the army, world leaders. I've tried everything I can think of. I see no other way of returning peace and stability. I'm desperate, beyond measure. I'm here because there is no other option. This country is on the verge of economic and social collapse.'

Wilson's eyes surveyed him coldly. They were unreadable. Dorne felt like Wilson was inside his head, hunting for lies.

Eventually Wilson said, 'I'll be honest, guv. I think you're telling me what I want to hear. But then, I don't know you – just what the media tells me about you. I don't trust you. But I don't trust them neither.' He pulled a cigar from a desk drawer, sniffed it and lit it. 'I don't trust no one.'

'A wise ethos.'

'Want one?' Wilson asked, holding forth his cigar.

Dorne shook his head.

Wilson looked out of the window and puffed smoke rings for a while. Then he said, 'I'll grant you an audience with Sea Beard. He can decide.'

'Thank you.'

Wilson raised his glass. 'To the future, and to the past. It's time for a gathering, under the dead ship's mast.'

Something about the way Wilson spoke the rhyme unnerved Dorne. The words felt like they held a hidden meaning that was binding. Absolute.

Wilson drank his rum and looked at Dorne.

If there were another option, Dorne thought, *I would not be here*. He gulped his drink.

'Follow me, guv,' said Wilson. 'We got a journey to make.'

4

Wilson led Dorne out of his office. They walked through clean corridors, then doors that required keys. They descended stairways that seemed unending, until the air smelt stale. The corridors became dustier, unused. There were no windows. No signs declaring 'EXIT'.

Aged lights flickered. The doorways were metal now, and required Wilson to look into camera lenses with one eye, then the other, before they would open.

More corridors. Another descending stairway. Now they were in a tunnel that disappeared into darkness. Wilson rummaged in an alcove, removed a lantern, lit it and grinned at Dorne. It was a chilling grin, wreathed in flickering shadows. 'Not far now, guv.'

They continued, crouching beneath a crumbling, cave-like ceiling. *Is this why Wilson stoops?* Dorne wondered. The air was warm and he felt claustrophobic, trapped, far below the ground with a man who appeared more unnerving the longer Dorne spent in his company.

They turned a corner. Dorne felt a welcome gust of cooler air as they emerged into a colossal hallway, its roof supported by pillars of swirling water. Sea life floated within the pillars – fish, squid, eels – watching him.

Something felt wrong. This place was alien. Of another time. Another place. They didn't belong here. Dorne felt nauseous. He bent over and retched.

'It's normal to feel detached when walking between worlds,' said Wilson. 'Rest for a moment. It'll pass.'

Dorne sat heavily on the floor, took a breath and looked around. At the far end of the hallway was an arch, decorated with carvings of sea serpents and other demons of the ocean. Protruding from the archway was the prow of a huge ship. It was chained to a colossal anchor that was half buried in the stone floor of the hallway. Dorne could hear water lapping in the gloom.

Wilson helped Dorne to his feet and led him towards the ship. The muzzles of cannon protruded from windows in the hull. Beneath them, the words 'The Stopped Clock' were painted on the wood in faded lettering.

A rope ladder dangled over the side of the ship.

'Sea Beard will be waiting on the deck,' said Wilson 'Be wary, guv. He's dangerous.'

As are you, thought Dorne, and started to climb.

5

Clambering onto the prow of the ship, Dorne emerged from under the archway into an alien world and fought the urge to run. He had to see this through. For his people.

Black stars shimmered in a grey sky. Dorne didn't recognise any of the constellations. With a shiver, he forced his eyes back down towards the deck. There were barrels, ropes, cannon balls, all neatly arranged. Five tall masts supported rotting sails.

Dorne walked forward. At the stern of the boat was the ship's wheel. Next to it stood a lone figure, looking out over the sea.

As Dorne approached, the figure turned around. He was dressed like a pirate from a fairy-tale and wore a tricorne, beneath which writhed a mass of squid-like tentacles. A patch covered one eye; his other was tawny, flecked with gold, just like Wilson's. His skin looked weathered and colourless, giving him an undead pallor. His beard was of the sea, moving like an ocean. Waves rolled away from the upper part of his face, their crests white, forming curling edges to his beard that looked like they should drip away. Somehow, the water defied gravity.

'Welcome aboard.' The pirate's voice sounded as if an ocean resided in his mouth. 'What brings you to *The Stopped Clock*?'

Is this real? thought Dorne. *Has my desperation sent me mad?*

'Staring is regarded as rude, even here.'

'I'm sorry,' Dorne replied. 'I was reading a book about you. It didn't…' He paused, to consider tact. 'The way you were described didn't do you justice.'

'All stories become twisted over time.' Despite the way he looked, the pirate exuded a calm authority. He waited patiently, giving Dorne a few moments to compose himself.

'I'm Charles Ernest Dorne, I'm the…' He stopped, wondering if job titles and places on Earth would mean anything here. 'I am the political leader of my country.'

'I am Sea Beard, Custodian of Time. What do you

want from me?'

Dorne recounted the story he'd told Wilson and finished by saying, 'I need to be murdered, in the past.'

Sea Beard waved a hand dismissively. 'I'm an observer. A truth seeker. I don't meddle with history. I merely see it.'

'Do you refrain from meddling because it's impossible? Or through choice?'

'It's a choice,' Sea Beard admitted. 'The ramifications of toying with time, even the minutest detail, can tear reality apart. When that happens, the walls that protect the living crumble. Doorways open, allowing life and death to collide.' With a wry smile, he added, 'It isn't a sensible thing to do.'

'Do you have a price?' Before Sea Beard could protest, Dorne quickly added, 'I apologise for being so direct, I mean no disrespect. I had to ask. I'll do anything in my power to gain your help.'

The glower forming on Sea Beard's face dissipated. 'Anything?'

'Yes.'

'Desperation makes fools of us all.' Sea Beard walked to the edge of the deck and looked out over a still sea. 'I do not dwell here by choice.'

'I'm sorry, I don't understand.'

Sea Beard turned, lifting his eye patch, revealing a scarred, empty socket. 'Wilson took it. His eye doesn't just look like mine. It is mine. It's how he controls me, keeps me prisoner and walks between worlds.'

'Controls you?'

'He called you 'guv', I'm guessing. Fed you rum.' Dorne nodded. 'You aren't the first to underestimate him. He's dangerous.'

'He said the same about you.'

'I'm sure he did. If I do what you ask, you must agree to free me.'

'How?'

'Reclaim my eye.' Sea Beard moved towards Dorne and looked down into his upturned face. 'Tear it from Wilson's skull.'

'I don't know if I could. Look at me, I'm no fighter.'

'Find a way.'

'If I manage to steal back your eye, do you promise to do as I have asked?'

'I will toy with time on your behalf.'

'It seems we are both desperate.'

Sea Beard smiled, revealing barnacled teeth. 'The wants and needs of men and demons are not so dissimilar.'

'Then we have an agreement.'

Dorne offered his hand. Sea Beard grabbed it and pulled. Dorne stumbled forwards and Sea Beard grabbed his face. His touch was cold and wet. He opened his mouth and Dorne saw his tongue, like his beard, was of the sea.

Paralysed, Dorne felt the pirate's beard lapping at his face, stinging his eyes. 'A deal has been done, under the dead ship's mast. The agreement is binding, in our souls it is cast.'

Salty water filled Dorne's mouth and ran down his throat. As he fought the urge to vomit, everything turned black.

6

Dorne opened his eyes. He was lying on a dusty Chesterfield sofa in Wilson's office. The room was full of shadows, dimly lit by flickering candles. His mouth tasted of sea water.

Dorne sat up and saw Wilson watching him from behind the desk.

'How'd it go, guv?'

'We reached an agreement.'

'Good. That means we need to discuss payment.' Wilson stood up, poured a glass of water from a decanter, walked around his desk and offered Dorne the drink.

Dorne took the glass gratefully. 'What do I owe you?'

'You tell me, guv. What did Sea Beard ask for?'

Dorne sipped the water. 'A favour.'

'What favour?'

'He didn't say. He wanted time to consider his options.'

'You ain't a very good liar, guv.'

'I don't know what you—'

Wilson grabbed Dorne by the neck and pulled him to his feet. Their faces were just inches apart. 'If he kills you, how's he going to call in that favour? And what's in it for me? No, guv. You owe me, not him.' The flickering candlelight accentuated the shadows around Wilson's eyes. 'You can start by telling me the truth.'

Dorne felt Wilson's grip tightening. 'Can't breathe,' he spluttered.

Wilson let go. As Dorne sucked air into his lungs, a punch came quick and unexpected. Dorne fell backwards and instantly felt the weight of Wilson on top of him.

'What favour?' Wilson snarled.

'I don't know. He didn't say.'

Wilson punched him again. There was a snapping sound and Dorne felt searing pain in his nose. 'Sea Beard's like a dog. You got to kick him sometimes, remind him who's boss.' Wilson lowered his face, until Dorne could taste the rum on his breath. 'Take something he wants away from him.'

Through watering eyes, Dorne could see murder on Wilson's face. And Sea Beard's eye, his key to redemption, tantalisingly close.

'Last chance,' said Wilson. 'What did he ask for?'

Dorne grabbed Wilson's head with both hands. Wilson flinched, but wasn't fast enough. Dorne's mouth encircled his left eye socket in a gruesome kiss. Wilson tried to pull away, but Dorne had a firm grip. He sucked hard. His mouth was suddenly full of eyeball, disgusting and slimy on his tongue. Dorne bit hard, severing the optic nerve. Wilson fell away from him screaming.

Dorne sat up and retched, spitting the eyeball out. Wilson clawed for the eye, but his skin was weathering, becoming tighter, restricting his movements. To Dorne, it looked like years were passing in seconds. Then Wilson's body disintegrated into a pool of water.

Dorne slumped backwards, exhausted.

7

Dorne drifted between dreams and reality. Shadows danced in his mind and the sound of oceans echoed in his ears.

He woke, bathed in sweat, as chimes resonated from the grandfather clock in the corner of Wilson's office.

The pain in his nose had become a dull ache. Feeling lightheaded, he slowly pulled himself into a sitting position. Candles, burning low, guttered and spat as cool night air filled the room from the open window.

'I will do well on this planet, where the ice is melting, transferring its power to the sea.'

Sea Beard was standing by the door, watching him. He looked more colourful than before. His clothes seemed rich and vibrant, but his skin remained pallid, devoid of life. And he still wore an eye patch.

Dorne saw the eyeball on the floor, in a puddle of water. The severed optic nerve twitched, as if alive.

'Why haven't you taken it?' Dorne asked.

'You must give it to me.'

'I will, when you've done as we agreed.'

'I already have.'

'I'm still alive.'

'Murder is rarely the best way to solve a problem.'

'So what did you do?' Dorne asked.

'Changed one word in a document you signed.'

'Was that enough?'

Sea Beard walked across the room and helped Dorne to his feet. 'Look outside.'

Dorne moved towards the window. The blue light of dawn illuminated tall glass buildings. They stood like futuristic sentinels over the city. No fires burned. There was no sign of malcontent. The streets below seemed peaceful.

'Will anyone remember how things were?'

'No. This building is the only place on Earth that can be everywhen at once. Only you and I will remember.'

'Thank you,' said Dorne, his voice trembling. Tears filled his eyes, despair replaced by relief. 'Thank you, so very much.'

'May I have my eye back?'

Dorne gathered himself and scooped up the eye. Instead of offering it to Sea Beard, he hesitated.

'You're wondering if you have to give it to me,' said Sea Beard, 'if you can control me, like Wilson.'

'I am. But the rhyme you spoke, it felt like an oath. Binding and irrevocable.'

'It was.'

'So, why do I feel like there's something you're not telling me?'

'Give me my eye.'

'No.' Dorne closed his fingers around the eyeball. 'Tell me.'

A glower settled on Sea Beard's face. 'You are no longer a world leader.'

Dorne felt his relief replaced by concern. 'Then what am I?'

'Nothing.'

'I don't understand.'

'The change I made resulted in a different path. You resigned, in disgrace. A more competent leader took your place.'

'This is not what we agreed.'

'We agreed that I would toy with time and you would retrieve my eye.'

Dorne felt like he was losing a game of chess. 'Cheat,' he spat.

'Fool,' Sea Beard countered. 'You have what you asked for. And your life. You should be thankful. Now give me what's mine.'

Dorne rushed towards the window, intending to fling the eye from it, but stopped himself. He might be angry – and Sea Beard was right, he had been foolish – but he wasn't stupid. He'd seen what happened to Wilson.

Dorne turned to face Sea Beard. 'I want Wilson's job.'

Sea Beard cocked his head. 'What makes you think Wilson had a job that needs doing?'

'You need this place. The location, it's important. What was it you said? "This building is the only place on Earth that can be everywhen at once." It needs maintaining. I can help.'

'No. You cannot.'

'Then I would rather renege on our agreement and face the consequences.' Dorne dropped the eyeball onto the floor and raised his foot above it.

'No,' Sea Beard shouted.

Dorne paused, lowering his heel, the ball of his foot hovering over the eye. 'Think quickly,' he said.

Sea Beard took a step towards Dorne. 'Do not try to control me.'

Dorne slowly lowered his foot until it rested on the eyeball, but Sea Beard didn't respond.

'I will do it,' said Dorne.

'And I won't stop you.'

It was Dorne's turn to think quickly. 'Very well,' he said. 'I will not seek to control you, if I can have the job.'

'I agree to your terms,' said Sea Beard.

Dorne picked up the eye and held out his hand. Sea Beard snatched it, placed the eye into his mouth, swallowed and then removed his eyepatch. Two tawny eyes, flecked with gold, stared at Dorne. Below them, the pirate's watery beard looked more vibrant, gleaming in the dawn light. Colour filled Sea Beard's face. No, Dorne discerned more than just colour. Health. Life.

Sea Beard poured a glass of rum. 'It has been so long since I lived. Breathed. Tasted.' He drank the rum, a look of joy on his face.

'What happens now?' Dorne asked.

'An oath must be spoken.'

'Then speak it.'

Sea Beard grabbed Dorne roughly, like he had on the boat. His beard lapped at Dorne's face as he spoke. 'An understanding is reached, on which we agree. Let he who reneges, face the wrath of the sea.'

As Sea Beard released his grip, unease crawled in Dorne's gut. He'd asked for death and received something else. Was he a fool to have demanded a job? 'Do you have any more surprises for me?'

Sea Beard poured two large glasses of rum and handed one to Dorne. 'I'm sure we both have plenty of surprises for one another, but they can wait.' He raised his glass and fixed Dorne with a twinkling stare. 'A toast. To the future, whatever it may hold.'

Dorne raised his glass. 'To the future, one I didn't think I'd have.'

They chinked their glasses and drank.

The rum left a warm trail down Dorne's gullet. As it sank towards his stomach, he realised he was enjoying the sensation. He moved to the window and looked at the view. The sun was rising and the future beckoned.

~

I AM THE
WARLOCK

1

I'm standing before a cavernous opening in a sheer rock face. The cave is cold, dark and ominous. Why are the locations for performing incantations of archaic sorcery always so inhospitable?

A sunny beach, in the shade of a palm tree – there's a good place to conduct magic. It's well lit, so you can see what you're doing with material spell components. Slippery rocks are easily avoided, so there's little danger of injury while performing the somatic elements. An abundance of plant and animal life can be found near a beach, and, more often than not, a plentiful supply of intoxicated virgins, all intrigued by talk of carnal rituals. Most magic, especially an invocation of summoning, requires all these resources to be readily available.

So, why must the location be at the top of a mountain, in a shadowy chamber, surrounded by a cave system where a monster is rumoured to dwell? It's an area where most plants can't survive, animals choose not to frequent and virgins definitely do not party.

I had to lug my virgin up here. In hindsight, I wish I'd selected a slimmer one. It's taken me three days and my legs are killing me. On top of that, I forgot my sacrificial blood-knife. Tonight is the full moon, so I don't have time to go back for it. Besides, what difference can the type of blade used to draw blood make? If you eat a fish with a steak-knife, it tastes just as good. Ancient scriptures always come with a long list of ridiculous stipulations.

'Are you going to kill me?' the virgin asks. Maybe arriving somewhere that looks like it offers an end to our journey has encouraged her to speak.

I find it best not to talk to them. They're like livestock. As soon as you give a chicken or a pig a name, it becomes hard to kill.

'My name is Wendy.'

Bollocks.

'I'd much rather know if you intend to try to hurt me so I can mentally prepare.'

I look at her, sitting in the snow beneath a pine tree, wrapped in a dirty burnoose, shivering. She isn't your stereotypical screaming kidnap victim. Her eyes are the grey of storm clouds and she speaks confidently, despite her situation. Her skin is pale, her lips full, her body curvaceous. Shit, now she has a name *and* I like the way she looks.

As I observe her, in what I hope is a rugged and dispassionate manner, I see disappointment on her face. Guilt compels me to speak.

'You see this cave?' I ask. She nods. 'It's sacred.'

I've never been much good at talking to women. The silence becomes uncomfortable before she says, 'And?'

'I have to perform an invocation of summoning, in the cave.'

'Have to?'

Oh yeah, absolutely do-or-die have to. All I say is, 'Yep.'

'Does it involve killing me?'

'Possibly.'

'Care to elaborate?'

'Depends how hungry the demon is.'

Tears glitter in her eyes. 'Fantastic.'

Not knowing how to deal with this, I bind her to the tree – the look she gives me suggests I may have chosen the incorrect course of action to appease her – and leave her to contemplate her fate, while I explore the cave.

Entering the shadows of the massive cavern, I discover it's lit by a pillar of sunlight, shining from a crevice high in the rooftop. Walking the cavern's edge, I see a sprawling mass of tunnels and fissures leading off in every conceivable direction.

Towards the back of the cavern, I find an abyss. This is where the chamber I seek is said to be situated. It's also where the Gordesian is rumoured to sleep. It's a myth, but seeing the vastness of the chasm before me gives the legend a plausible edge. Gooseflesh crawls up my neck. A gargantuan lizard might live down there.

I feel my over-active imagination stirring. Quickly, I turn away from the hole and remove my backpack. I rummage through its contents and find the map. Studying it, I try to ignore the fire-spewing dragon so beautifully depicted at the top of the parchment. To my left, I should find a stairway.

The cavern is dark, so I light a torch and walk carefully over the uneven surface. Thin white streaks lace the black granite beneath my feet. They glisten in the firelight.

Ahead, I see a thin set of slippery steps carved into a huge rock that juts over the chasm's edge. The stairway hangs precariously above the abyss, curving out of sight.

Not a particularly inspiring route for a man with the dexterity of a beached whale, but the stairs' existence proves I'm in the right place. Rather than climb them now, and then again with Wendy – crap, I mean the virgin – I decide to collect her before exploring further.

Emerging from the cave mouth, I find her looking south, over the lands of Gordesia. The morning haze has cleared, burnt off by the sun, and the view from this altitude is stunning, made all the more spectacular by the majesty of the surrounding mountain peaks.

'Lovely day,' I say.

She spits at me.

I untie her feet and lead her to the steps in the cavern.

'There's no way I'm climbing up there with my hands tied,' she says, her features accentuated by the dancing torchlight. There's a shit-or-bust glint in her eye that suggests I'd be unwise to release her.

'Sorry,' I say, and shove her ahead of me. She stumbles, but it looks orchestrated – there's a grace to her movements, like that of a dancer, which makes me think she's faking clumsiness.

The rocky steps are slippery and too shallow for my liking, making me uncomfortably aware of the drop beneath me. We move out around the overhang. Here, the climb becomes steeper. At the top of the steps I can see a carved opening in the rock from which a red light flickers.

Wendy has moved some way ahead of me now, but if I rush I might fall. I curse as I see her disappear into the fire-lit hole. I'm on my guard as I approach. If I were her, I'd use every opportunity to try to escape.

The steps lead to a natural ledge onto which the flickering entranceway opens. It's carved magnificently to look like the mouth of a dragon.

I take a breath, toss my torch into the abyss, and stride in. She's waiting and runs at me, trying to shoulder-charge me backwards off the ledge. I pre-empt her attack and her wrists are bound behind her – these two facts save me, for I'm no fighter. I sidestep, trip her, and she sprawls onto the ground. I grab her under the armpits, drag her upright and make her lead the way.

The passage is short, ending in a chamber that's maybe 20 metres square. It's full of twisted pillars and grotesque statues. At one end is a roaring fire, which I recognise to be magical in nature as it burns without fuel. It supplies some welcome heat after three days of exposure on the mountain. In the centre of the chamber stands a crumbling stone altar.

I bind the virgin's feet and watch as she takes in her surroundings. A tear trickles down her cheek. Feeling pangs of guilt, I unload my backpack, checking through the array of goods I've brought with me. I light more torches, placing them in the aged brackets which decorate the walls, before starting to draw the necessary runes on the altar in chalk and charcoal. All the time I'm careful to keep one eye on the virgin.

She watches me for a while and says, 'Why are you doing this?'

Because I was stupid and drunk enough to declare a challenge no sober man would ever consider. What I actually say is, 'Because I can.'

'Tosser,' she says.

The insult annoys me. 'Look, climbing a mountain with an unhappy virgin to sit in a cave and summon a demon isn't high on my list of priorities, but dying is even lower. As that's the alternative I'm faced with, here we are.'

I see her smirk.

'Why the face?' I ask.

'How much did you pay for me?'

'Five pieces of silver and a lump of cheese.'

133

'Cheese?' She seems offended.

'It was good cheese. Why did you ask?'

'I'm not a virgin.'

'What?'

'Actually, I'm a bit of a slag.'

I drop my chalk. A missing blood-knife is one thing, but no virgin... If by some miracle I do manage to entice a demon through the portals of time using my current itinerary, not only will it be of low intelligence, it'll be very unhappy with its supper. Dejected demons of any calibre are notoriously hard to appease. But my options are limited: possible death or certain death. At least the decision is easy.

Ignoring the wry smile on her face, I continue as though her promiscuity is only a minor setback. I pull a vial of red liquid from my pocket.

'Drink this please.'

'What is it?'

'An elixir made from rose petals, paprika, oil and opiates,' I say, neglecting to mention the lamb's blood, frog's spittle and hippo's... well... discharge. She doesn't look convinced. 'I can force you to drink it if you like,' I say, removing a tubular medical contraption from my bag that looks a little like a shoehorn. I purchased it in a market years ago. I've no idea what it was designed for, but something about its shape suggests the discomfort that could be caused if it were to be inserted into any of the orifices made available by the human anatomy. Its presence is usually enough to make people drink up. Today is no exception. She allows me to pour the liquid into her mouth and swallows.

As I move back to the altar and continue drawing, she asks, 'Why will you die if you don't summon a demon?' She's beginning to slur.

'I challenged Bane.'

'Bane the Warlock?'

'Yep.'

She sniggers. 'That was silly.'

I'm unable to disagree. I walk over to her with my knife, take her right hand and draw a spot of blood from the tip of her index finger. She's gone all floppy now and offers little resistance. I open a small wooden box and carefully remove the shed skin of a wolf spider. I dab this with her blood.

'Gross,' she slurs.

I ignore her and light some candles before placing the spider skin in the middle of a large circle in the glyph I've drawn on the altar. As soon as it touches the stone, the spider animates and scuttles around, never crossing the lines of the circle. I feel a release of tension; at least I got this part right.

I look back at Wendy. No, the virgin. Damn it, as near to a virgin as I could find. She's lying on her side, seemingly asleep and drooling. Good, she'd probably laugh at the next bit and put me off.

I strip naked, smear black and red paste onto my face and body in the required patterns, quickly consult the scriptures, and then begin to recite the verses, accompanied by the spiritual dance I've rehearsed. It takes about three hours. By the end I'm exhausted, but glad I had no audience to see my bits jiggling during some of the more exuberant lunges that the ritual demands. I slump into a heap before the altar and, just as I feel the tantalising fingers of sleep tickling my consciousness, I hear someone clear their throat behind me.

Looking up, I notice the stink of sulphur filling the room.

Before me stands a demon. It's 10, maybe 11 feet tall, and as it steps down from the altar it leaves black splodges scorched into the stone.

A crown of flaming horns protrudes from its scalp and its skin ripples with heat, as if its entire body is formed from volcanic lava. Writhing on its chin are hundreds of blackened vipers, forming a grotesque beard. The demon and the snakes regard me with eyes that twinkle like stars.

It stands for a while, as if expecting something from me. I'm too stunned to speak. I just sit there like an idiot, gawping in awe at the creature standing before me and wondering how I managed to summon it using a crappy dagger and a nymphomaniac. This is no young, stupid cacodemon. The thing standing before me must be some sort of demonic deity.

Eventually it speaks. 'It is customary, at this point of an invocation, to introduce yourself,' it says, with a voice as subtle as cannon-fire.

'Jacob,' I say, more shrilly than I intended.

'Generally, I would expect more bowing and graciousness,' it says, 'accompanied by offerings of... hospitality.'

I try to rein in my manners, standing and proffering a bow as courteously as a filthy, naked man can.

'Are you hungry?' I ask.

The demon looks beyond me, at the snoring Wendy. 'Think I'll give it a miss.'

'Sorry,' I say, intensely relieved.

'A practitioner of sorcery with a conscience. Interesting.'

I wonder if the demon can read my mind and feel a frown crease my brow.

'The human face often betrays more than its owner

might like,' it says. 'Do you know who you have summoned?'

'King of dead?' I venture.

The demon snorts laughter, forcing jets of fire to explode from the mouths of the snakes that form its beard. 'No,' it says. 'My name is Gee.'

'What's that short for?' I ask, assuming it'll be something horrific.

'Gabriel.'

I fail to hold back a snigger.

'I hope you've requested my presence for good reason, for names can be deceptive.'

Shit. Here's the moment of truth. 'I made a challenge to Bane the Warlock. It's a bit stupid really...'

'Do tell.'

'He was boasting about summoning demons, so I said I could summon a bigger demon than he could.' Dear lord, this sounds even more pathetic than I imagined. 'And that my demon could beat his up.'

Gee takes a step towards me and I feel the heat emanating from his body. 'Normally I'd kill you for wasting my time. And as you've defiled the purity of a princess, which is the only reason I'm obliged to be here, I'd claim your soul.'

Gee waits a moment while I complete the mental jigsaw-puzzle. 'Wendy's a...' He nods. 'I bought her for five silver pieces and a lump of cheese.'

'Bargain. As I was saying, regarding your soul...'

'Sorry.'

'Normally you'd be dead, but I have business with your opponent and he's been avoiding me for some considerable time. I assume you've preordained a suitable site for this demonic showdown?'

'Yes, there's an abandoned castle ruin at the base of

Mount Plissken.'

'Will there be an audience?'

If I thought I'd get to witness two demons doing battle and then see the sorcerer who summoned the loser condemned to damnation in eternal fire, I'd be there. 'Probably,' I say.

'Good,' says Gee. 'From witnesses, legends are born.' He claps his hands. I hear thunder rumble inside my head and then...

2

I'm in a cobbled courtyard that's bathed in starlight. Crumbling statues and ruined battle crenellations line its edges. The shadowed peaks of the Gordesian Mountains provide an imposing backdrop to the scene.

There's no sign of Gee, but there is a crowd of maybe 300 locals from nearby villages, all watching in quiet anticipation.

'Looking good.'

Turning to my left, I see Wendy lying on the ground, staring up at me. I'm suddenly conscious of being naked and covered in the filth of my sweat-smudged patterns, but there's sod all I can do, so I lob up a mental wall.

'Where are we?' she asks.

I don't have time to explain and feel as though I've brought enough jeopardy into her life for one day. 'This'll be dangerous,' I say, bending down and untying her bonds. 'You'd best bugger off.'

'How chivalrous.'

She rubs her wrists but doesn't stand. Her face is white with fatigue and I can see droplets of sweat coating her forehead.

'Did your demon show up?' she asks.

I nod. 'Yep.'

She inspects her limbs. 'No bite marks.'

'It wasn't hungry.'

'What if it gets peckish later? I'd hate to appear rude.'

'I don't think it found you all that appetising.'

She wipes the sweat from her brow with a trembling hand. 'Twat.'

A sudden explosion of light shreds the darkness, accompanied by the boom of time being torn apart.

Bane the Warlock appears at the other end of the courtyard amidst a flash of white flame. He's dressed in black and wrapped in a cloak of snakeskin. His jet-black hair is combed back tightly to his skull and his long, immaculately trimmed sideburns give him a wolf-like demeanour. He leans on an aged, oaken staff.

Behind him, squats an abomination that's about 20 feet tall. Black, scaled skin covers its gargantuan body, bull neck and reptilian head. Two misshapen wings extend from bony protrusions on its back, which it flexes while surveying me with opaque eyes. As it breathes, red mist seeps from its tusks.

Bane smiles thinly and nods at Wendy. 'This is supposed to be a battle of demons, not overfed bitches. Is this the best you can do, wizard?' He spits the last word like an insult.

'Nope,' I say, feeling strangely annoyed by him insulting Wendy. 'I've summoned a foe of worth.'

'Really?' says Bane. 'Show me.'

Gee chooses this moment to appear from behind a statue. I see a look of shock on Bane's face. 'How—'

'Jacob inadvertently used royal blood,' says Gee. 'How many virgins were required to summon that?' He nods at the mammoth demon, which is still squatting behind Bane.

'One or two,' says Bane.

'Four,' says the demon, its voice sibilant.

'Thank you,' says Gee, looking up at the abomination. 'I assume you'd rather be returned to your location of origin than fight me?'

The thing nods its head. Gee points at the floor. Lightning sizzles and a gaping black mouth opens in the cobbles beneath the demon, swallowing it. I notice that the crowd are watching as though Medusa has done a quick run around and subjected them all to a glare in the eyes.

Gee turns his attention to Bane. 'Balance,' he says. 'You remember our agreement regarding the maintenance of balance?'

Although there's a glower of defiance residing in his eyes, Bane looks like a scared old man. Despite myself, I feel sorry for him. I remember one of the more eloquent moments from the drunken confrontation that resulted in this stupid wager. I told Bane that his cruelty invited damnation. Being proved right isn't as satisfying as I'd imagined.

'You swore an oath,' Gee continues, 'the breach of which carries a penalty.'

'I remember,' says Bane.

'With those gathered to bear witness, I invoke the will of the staff.'

Bane licks his lips and I see greed in his eyes. 'I will not relinquish my position willingly,' he says.

Gee shrugs. 'Staff of the Warlock, make your judgement.'

I see the oaken staff in Bane's hand flash with green light. Shocked, possibly burnt, Bane releases his grip.

The staff falls to the ground where I see it shoot tiny branches and sprout leaves. Some of this new growth twists to form wooden claws, which the staff uses to scrabble quickly across the cobbles. Initially, I think it's heading towards Gee, but it crawls past him towards me.

No.

No way.

Responsibility is definitely not my thing.

I can barely...

The staff veers away from me and crawls towards Wendy, coming to rest at her feet. Relief and jealousy make an unlikely alliance in my gut. I feel like I might puke.

'She's not worthy,' Bane shrieks. 'The power cannot go to a woma—'

Bane's head explodes. Gore spatters in every direction. I'm unsure if Gee or the oaken staff is responsible. Wendy looked like she wanted him to shut up too. Could it have been her? I hope not, or when this is over my life expectancy will be similar to that of a mayfly.

I glance at Gee, who's standing there, melting the ground beneath his feet. He looks at Wendy and says, 'I would hand you the staff, but it's probably combustible.'

She stands unsteadily. Her forehead is moist with fresh perspiration and her limbs are shaking. The combination of opiates and the unmentionable liquids collected from hippos isn't all that good for your kidneys.

She picks up the staff. It looks like it belongs in her hand. In Bane's possession, it appeared dead. Now, with leaves and tiny acorns dangling from its new protrusions, it seems complete.

Gee moves to stand before us.

'You're not a demon?' I ask. Gee shakes his head. 'You look like a demon.'

'Looks can be deceptive.'

'So, who are you?'

'A servant of balance.' He looks at Wendy. 'As now are you. You will be responsible for the power you hold. You must maintain harmony. To accept this position means accepting responsibility. To neglect said responsibility, when challenged by myself, forfeits your position and your soul to the will of the staff. Will you swear the oath?'

'I am the Warlock,' says Wendy. She looks surprised, as if the words sprung from her mouth uninvited.

Gee nods. 'Good.' He looks at the gathered crowd. 'Bow,' he commands. They do so. 'The show's over. Leave.' The crowd seems happy to oblige. Shortly, only Gee, Wendy and I remain.

'You will serve her,' says Gee, the eyes of his snake-beard dazzling me. 'You will act as council on concerns of balance.'

I'm unsure that he's making the wisest of choices. Judging by the look gracing Wendy's face, I guess she is in full agreement with me, but neither of us deems it wise to voice an argument.

'You're the boss,' I say.

He nods in approval. 'It's time for me to leave.'

I don't want him to go, not yet. I'm unprepared. I don't really know what's expected of me. What I say is, 'What about virgins?'

'What about them?' says Gee.

'I mean, using them...' This is coming out all wrong. I decide to start again. 'What about utilising blood offerings in sorcery? Even rituals meant to do good require sacrifice of sorts.'

'It's recognising when oblation is acceptable for the greater good.' I receive Gee's smouldering stare one last time. 'It's all about balance.'

There's a flash of blackness and Gee is gone.

'Wendy the Warlock,' I mutter, with a hint of envy. 'I didn't know you were a princess and a sorceress.'

'I've studied sorcery,' she says, 'more closely than you, by the looks of it.' There's a lack of conviction in her scorn. I notice moistness around her eyes. She looks uncertain and scared. 'How can I take on this responsibility? The power I possess...' She falters. 'Look what happened to Bane.'

'Possess is the wrong word,' I say. 'You're just a guardian. You don't own the power. You just have to babysit it.'

I intended that to be an insult, but she smiles at me. 'Thank you.'

I'll never understand women.

'You're shivering,' she says.

'I'm naked and it's cold.'

'Then let's find you some clothes.' She starts to walk from the courtyard.

'Then what?' I ask.

She turns around, leaning on the staff. The moistness on her brow has dried and her colour is returning. 'We'll talk about balance.'

The answer seems so obvious now she's said it. Who'd have thought it? Wendy really is the Warlock.

She turns and walks from the courtyard.

And I follow.

~

144

THE DAY MY PRAYERS WERE ANSWERED

hat's your name, friend?'

'James.'

'James what?'

'Blake.'

Yes, my name's James Blake. I'm tied to a chair in a grotty cellar, being questioned by Seth 'Cannon' Harris.

'Where do you live, James Blake?'

'Bristol.'

His questions are asked nicely enough, with a patient smile. 'Whereabouts?'

'Redland.'

'You know, James, I don't like asking three questions to get one answer.'

He wants my address?

'Are you ignoring me now?' He leans forward, his jacket flopping open, revealing a holstered gun.

'Flat six, 73 Haven Hill, BS6 7ZH. Please don't hurt my dog.'

'That's better,' says Cannon. 'So, James, where's the money?'

'It's gone.'

I can't lie. I've heard the whispered tales about those stupid enough to bullshit Cannon Harris – how they accidentally shoot themselves in the head, using his gun.

'Gone?'

I nod. 'Sorry.'

He's known as Cannon because of the Smith & Wesson model 500 Magnum revolver he carries, and because of rumours about the thing in his pants that allegedly keeps a wife, mistress, girlfriend and other random conquests coming back for more.

'Gone where?'

'I spent it.'

This isn't strictly true, but it's true enough. I doubt he'd believe what actually happened to the money. I can barely believe it myself.

'Adams wants it back.'

'The cash belonged to Clive Adams?' This makes what happened to the money even more unbelievable. 'I'd never have taken it if—'

'Can you get it back?'

'No.'

That was the wrong thing to say. He looks detached.

'I mean, yes,' I say. 'Just not right now. Please, give me a week. I'll get the money.'

'I don't do gifts, James.'

Cannon reaches inside his jacket.

I know I'm not religious, but right now, Lord, I could do with your help. I think Cannon is going to blow a hole in my head. No great loss, I know, but if you can hear me, please, please do something. I'll do anything you ask. My eyes roll upwards and I whisper, 'Please, help me.'

'Are you praying?' Cannon smiles. 'I've seen people pray before, James.' He draws the Magnum and screws a homemade silencer into place. 'It never stops what will be.'

I close my eyes. This is it. Three grand seemed so important when I nicked it. Worth any risk, any consequence. Cannon should be a counsellor. He's put everything into perspective for me. I can see what's important now. Three grand ain't it. If you help me, Lord, I'll stop being such a dick. I'll change. 'Please, God, please.'

'God needs an ENT appointment, James.' I hear the click of the hammer being pulled back. 'Any last words?'

I smell burning. Like an electric socket has blown. An electric socket that was powering a star.

'That time again.' The voice is musical, in a disgruntled way. 'Fabulous.'

I open my eyes. The grotty cellar is now lit with a maroon glow. The source of the light is a hairless being wearing a beautifully woven cloak of black silk. I can't tell if it's male or female. The face is beautiful, yet alien; smooth skinned and elfish. Its skin is golden, its musculature powerful, its limbs long. Claws protrude from the tips of its fingers and toes. I can see bat-like wings folded behind broad shoulders. Its smile is even harder to read than Cannon's. We could be in the company of an angel, a demon, or something in-between. Whatever it is, my life expectancy has been extended, so I'm pleased to see it.

'Looks like we have an interesting situation here,' the being says.

'Who... *What* are you?' asks Cannon.

'I don't like your tone,' it replies.

Cannon points his gun at the being. 'Whatever you are, this'll hurt.'

Cannon pulls the trigger. The Magnum fires. The bullet hits the being in the chest. It doesn't rip a hole in its body. It doesn't shatter or ricochet. The shell just drops to the floor, tinkling on the stone like a fumbled penny.

'Let's get this over with,' says the being. 'I'm Angel. You're Cannon. This is James. I'm here to mediate. Put the gun away or I'll make your most coveted body part a memory.'

Cannon fires the gun again, this time at me. It happens so fast that I don't have time to think. I feel the bullet gently nudge the skin of my forehead, then it drops to the floor, same as before.

'If you put the gun away, when this is over, you can have your cock back,' says Angel.

Cannon fumbles at his crotch. 'You bast—'

'Insult me and it'll return deformed, inoperative, incurably disease ridden... My choices are endless.'

I can see fury prowling in Cannon's eyes. A resigned fury, like that of a predator who's had his kill snatched by the alpha male. Angel smiles revealing endless rows of tiny serrated teeth as Cannon holsters his gun. This gives me enough time to realise that a bullet just bounced off my forehead. I should be dead. I start to hyperventilate.

'Paper bag,' I manage, between gasps.

'There's no time for placebos.' Angel touches my shoulder. Instantly the panic subsides. And the ropes that bind me to the chair wither and fall to the floor. 'Better?'

'Are you an angel?' I ask.

'An angel called Angel? Please.'

'So, what are you?'

'An incubus.'

'You don't have any horns,' I say.

'Very observant. Well done.'

'But on Wikipedia—'

'Yes, yes, I've seen it,' says Angel. 'A very imaginative entry filled with legends, myths and artists' impressions, but somewhat lacking in the departments of photographic evidence and fact.'

I glance at Cannon. I see him pinch the back of his hand and mutter a curse.

'You're not mad,' says Angel. 'I'm real and I have somewhere to be. Can we get on with this?'

'Get on with what?' says Cannon.

'I'm here to mediate, until the situation is resolved.'

'Why?'

'Two reasons. One, it would be inconvenient if James were to die. Two—'

'Inconvenient?' I spit. 'That's an understatement if you ask me.'

'I didn't.'

I'm about to speak again, but a glower settles on Angel's face, which makes me opt for silence.

'Very wise,' says Angel. 'May I continue?'

I nod.

'Like I said, two reasons. One, inconvenience. Two, there are laws beyond your comprehension regarding balance. They must be honoured. In simplistic terms, to believe in good is to believe in evil. So evil has to put in as many appearances as good for belief to receive a healthy, sustainable diet. Balance, you see?'

'Not really,' says Cannon.

I think I get it. 'You answered my prayer to prove your existence,' I say, feeling honoured, and a little bit smug.

'Yes,' says Angel. 'To him.' He nods at Cannon.

'You're here for Cannon? He doesn't believe in gods.'

'Exactly.'

'Neither do I.'

'You believed enough to pray.'

'OK, consider me converted,' says Cannon. 'What now?'

Angel gives Cannon a thin smile. 'Tell me what happened,' he says.

'James nicked three grand off Clive Adams,' says Cannon.

'Is this true, James?' asks Angel.

'Yes.'

'It's my job to get it back, with interest,' says Cannon. 'Payment options are cash or blood.'

'Seems fair enough,' says Angel. 'James?'

'I don't have it.'

'Says he spent it,' says Cannon.

'This true too, James?' asks Angel.

'Sort of,' I say.

'Sort of?'

Here we go. 'My cousin gave me an errand to deliver three grand to a warehouse on the docks. I didn't know he was working for Adams, I just thought he was being fat and lazy. Well, he was, but I didn't know.'

'Scene set,' says Angel. 'And?'

'I already had a debt. To Adams. This is where it all gets a bit crazy...'

'I like crazy,' says Angel.

'I borrowed a grand off Adams to pay a gambling debt six months back,' I continue. 'With interest, I owe him three. I was going to use the money my cousin gave me to pay Adams back and tell my cousin I'd been mugged.'

'So you stole money *from* Adams to pay off your debt *to* Adams?'

'I didn't know that at the time, but yes,' I say. 'I went to Adams's place, to give him the money, but he wasn't there so I left it with Monkey. Long story short, Monkey says he never saw me that day and now I'm six grand down.'

'You trusted a man called Monkey?' asks Angel.

I nod.

'That's special, James,' says Angel, transferring his gaze to Cannon. 'I'm beginning to see why you wanted him dead.'

'But you're here to save me,' I say.

'No, I'm here to mediate. And while it would be inconvenient for you to die, it wouldn't be the end of the world.'

'That's the last time I pray for help,' I mutter.

Angel looks at Cannon. 'You think three grand becoming six is fair?'

'I don't really care,' says Cannon.

'It seems to me that James owes Adams three grand,' says Angel, pulling a wad of money from inside his cloak, 'plus an extra 250 for the inconvenience caused. If I give you this, I feel the situation is resolved. Agreed?'

'OK, agreed,' says Cannon.

I can't believe an incubus wouldn't spot Cannon's insincerity.

Angel proffers a clawed hand to Cannon, who hesitates for a moment, then shakes it. I see a strange look appear on Cannon's face as their hands meet, like the incubus's touch is causing him pain.

'A handshake is binding, Seth Harris,' says Angel. 'Never forget it. Your cherished bits are back, but I can't promise how long they'll hang around, if you'll pardon the pun.' Angel looks back at me. 'My work here is done. James, Cannon, it's been a pleasure.' He pauses. 'Actually, no. More of a chore.'

'Hang on,' I say. 'You're just going to leave me here with him?'

'Yes.'

'He might kill me.'

'Indeed he might.'

'But I'm convenient. You said so.'

'You have a purpose, in too many possible futures to ignore. Like I said, it would be inconvenient if you die, not disastrous.'

'What is this purpose?'

'If you live, check your pockets.' The smell of stars intensifies. 'And remember your prayer.'

Angel disappears. No blinding flash, no deafening whoosh, he's just gone, like a dream on waking.

I turn to face Cannon. He's watching me intently.

'You know,' says Cannon, 'when Adams finds out all that happened, he'll still want another three grand. Plus interest.'

'And you know where I live,' I say.

'Yeah.' His eyes are cold, but there's something new about his manner. I think Angel might have succeeded in both his reasons for being here. He's made Cannon think.

'Thing is,' Cannon continues, 'I can't remember what number York Road you said. It was York, right?' He looks me up and down. 'Get out of here, James Blake.'

I don't need telling twice. I run out of the door, along a corridor, up some stairs, out into a back alley and onto a busy street. People bustle around me. I pull my hood up and lose myself in the crowd, finding comfort in the safety of rush-hour's hubbub.

I stuff my hands deep in my hoodie's pocket. My fingers touch something cold and hard. I remember Angel's parting words.

I see a park and find a bench in a secluded corner. Sitting down, I pull the object from my pocket. It's a silver coin. Lifting the coin close to study it, I notice the faint smell of stars. On the front is a picture of a demon wreathed in fire. It winks at me and the coin flips over all on its own. There's an inscription on the back. It reads:

From Angel
To James
From James
To Cannon

That's my purpose? No one can help a psycho like Cannon, least of all a tit like me.

Then I remember my prayer and silent vow. I said I'd do anything.

'You should be gone, James.'

I spin around. Cannon is standing behind me. I see a bronze aura surrounding his body, but it's tainted by a corrupt blackness that radiates from the gun. Now I possess demonic-coin-o-vision. Fabulous.

'Did you drug me?' he asks. I try to answer but he cuts me off. 'I'm not hallucinating anymore, James.'

Cannon draws his gun. My sphincter twitches.

'Found a coin,' I blurt.

'Lucky you.'

'Look,' I say, standing up and showing it to him, 'on the back it says—'

Before I can finish, Cannon raises his gun and shoots me in the face.

2

I'm still standing, but my body is lying on the floor. I watch Cannon bend down and take the coin from my dead hand. He reads the legend on the back. The colour drains from his face and the gun slips from his fingers. As it falls to the floor, the aura around his body changes from bronze to burning gold.

'It really was all about him.'

'I did say so.'

I look around and see Angel standing next to me.

'Did I fulfil my purpose?' I ask.

'Yes,' says Angel.

'I thought I might get to live a bit longer.'

'Why?'

I have no answer.

I go back to watching Cannon, who seems oblivious to our presence. He picks up the Magnum and stares at it contemplatively for a moment before holstering it. Although the gun still radiates blackness, its touch no longer corrupts the golden aura that surrounds him. He walks away, head down.

'What happens now?'

'Cannon's path is important. He has a better chance of fulfilling his destiny.'

'I meant to me.'

Angel reaches out and his claws tear a slash in the air. Beyond is blackness. 'After you, James.'

I don't know where he's taking me, but his tone suggests I have no option. Whatever awaits, the last few hours of my life suggest it'll be interesting.

With trepidation, I step into darkness.

~

THE KEITH OF DEATH

'm in Debenhams' menswear department, trying to work out if the rhino is real. I've been self-medicating for my headaches and, I admit, sometimes I can be a little overzealous with my dosage. The tablets look like Skittles and, well, I like Skittles.

The rhino is grazing on socks, snarling, revealing more pointed teeth than you'd expect to find in a herbivore. Its skin is white and its body shimmers like a glacier in the sun. Black tendrils of electricity fizz around its horn.

I've almost convinced myself that the rhinoceros is a hallucination, when I feel a hand on my arm.

'Is that a rhino?'

I glance to my left and see a dude clasping a selection pack of boxer shorts so tightly that his knuckles look like alabaster.

'You can see it too?' I ask.

He nods.

We both gawp at the rhino, transfixed.

I'm just beginning to think the rhino is real when a thought occurs to me. Maybe the dude is a figment of my imagination too? I turn to study him.

He's middle-aged and rotund, built like a beach ball. Beads of sweat glisten above his googly eyes and his nasal hair is mesmerising; every time he breathes out it dances like seaweed in a neap tide. Hmm. He looks real. How can I be sure? I punch him in the arm, harder than I intended. He stumbles sideways.

'What the...?' He regains his balance and punches me in the face. It hurts. He's definitely real.

As I dab at the blood trickling from my nose, I see the rhino rise onto its hind legs and walk towards us. With each step it takes, threads of ice crawl from its feet, clawing at the floor tiles like they're alive.

The rhino growls. My balls tingle. This feels very real and very amiss. Still, me and Punchy both stand there, hypnotised. Are you supposed to be aggressive and try to look big when facing a rhino, like you would a bear? Or cower? Or run? Are there different rules when the rhino can walk on its hind legs? I don't remember David Attenborough dealing with any of this.

The rhino stops its advance and looks through us with dead eyes. 'Keith,' it says, nodding at me. 'Desmond.' It nods at Punchy. 'Two at once. What fun.' Its voice is guttural.

'Wha'?' I manage, after the silence becomes uncomfortable.

'I'm the Rhino of Death,' says the Rhino of Death. 'You're both dead.'

'Wha'?' says Desmond.

'Take as long as you need,' says the rhino.

It turns out me and Punchy Des need a substantial amount of time.

I look around. I see a body lying in the bra aisle. Wait. Not a body. My body (I came in here for socks, but the menswear department is right next to the womenswear department and, well, I like bras). It's not just my body; it's my body with a stiletto sticking out of its skull. Punchy Des's body is in the same state next to a rack of boxer shorts.

'What happened to us?' I ask.

'You're the first victims of the Stiletto Psycho,' says

the Rhino of Death, 'a killer destined to be more famous than Jack the Ripper. Your murders will be dramatized by the BBC for centuries.'

'Lucky us.'

'Quite.'

'So, is this heaven?' asks Punchy Des.

'Debenhams' menswear department?' The rhino chuckles, causing icy flakes to rise from its nostrils. They twinkle eerily in the artificial lighting. 'No.'

'So, what happens now?' I ask.

'We must race.' There's an unpleasant glint in the rhino's black eyes. It's toying with us. 'If you win, eternity will be yours.'

'And if we lose?'

A white, forked tongue flickers between the rhino's teeth. 'You will be mine.'

I have the distinct feeling that wouldn't be good. 'Where do we race to?'

'Well, "race" is probably the wrong word,' says the Rhino of Death. '"Hunt" might be more appropriate.'

'Hunt?'

'It works like this. You run. I'll count to ten. Then I'll try to find you.'

Debenhams usually feels so calm and relaxing. So normal. Today, it feels demonic. The air is freezing and my core feels cold, like my soul is being stalked. I'm not a crier, but I feel a tear run down my cheek. The thought of playing a child's game with this creature seems terrifying.

I look at Punchy Des. He's in a worse state than me. In addition to tears, snot hangs from his nose, dampening his nasal-mane's hypnotic dance. 'This isn't what's supposed to happen when you die,' he says.

'What is?' The rhino's smile is devoid of empathy.

'I dunno,' he says. 'But not this.'

'If you think life was unfair, wait until you better understand death.' The rhino takes a step towards us. The cold radiating from the creature is so intense it hurts. 'I'd start running if I were you.' The rhino turns his back on us. 'Ten.'

Punchy Des gawps at me.

'Nine.'

Des turns and runs, knocking over a mannequin dressed in revealing red underwear, before getting on the up escalator. Up? I'd have chosen down. Maybe that's what the rhino expects. Go, Punchy Des, be luckier in death than you were in life.

'Eight.'

I'm not a big fan of running. I lack the coordination to do anything gracefully, especially at speed.

'Seven.'

And I'm pretty sure running is pointless. There was a glint in the rhino's eyes that suggested the hunt was a formality, the game had already been won.

'Six.'

I look around for a weapon. There's lots of men's clothing. None of it could really be used effectively to attack anyone. Or in defence. I could go and find a stiletto. Even that wouldn't be much use against an undead rhinoceros.

'Five.'

I could hide. But where? I have a feeling hiding would be even less use than running. Standing there with its back to me, the rhino looks like a smoke machine that's malfunctioned. Icy fog billows from its shoulders.

'Four.'

I reach into my pocket, pull out my fags and light

one. Well, I wasn't expecting that to work. Apparently being dead sucks in every way imaginable, but you can still smoke.

'Three.'

I take a long drag and study the perfectly formed cylinder of smoky wonderment held between my thumb and forefinger. I purse my lips and blow smoke at my fag. Ash crumbles from the end, revealing a glowing tip.

'Two.'

I look at the rhino. The cold rhino. And then back at my cigarette. My hot cigarette.

'One.'

I take one more drag. I'm not the hunted. I'm the hunter. And my weapon is a cigarette. A cigarette... A small tube of leaves, smouldering at one end. Hmm. I feel my confidence wane. I probably should've run.

'Ready or not, here I come.'

The Rhino of Death spins around. As it sees me standing there, holding my fag like a dagger, the rhino goes from looking all deranged and psycho, like Jack Nicholson busting through that door in *The Shining*, to shocked by something completely unexpected, like the crew of the Nostromo when that baby alien explodes out of John Hurt's chest.

The rhino falters. I stab at it with my cigarette. I'm lucky; the ciggy strikes, the tip sizzling on the base of the rhino's horn.

Its mouth opens. It's like a shark's. There are thousands of teeth in there, all serrated and gleaming. I think the rhino is going to bite my head off when a high-pitched noise emits from the hole my cigarette left in its horn. I think my ears might explode, but then the rhino explodes instead, into an icy mist. Its horn is all that remains intact. It thuds on the floor.

My cigarette has gone soggy. I discard it and light another. I'm not used to winning, especially that easily. I'm surprised to find I gain no pleasure from it.

I wonder if all of this is just the meds. I've always had a vivid imagination. It tends to get out of control when I'm stimulated. By anything.

I reach into the lingering mist and touch the rhino's horn. It's unbelievably cold. My fingers turn white, like snow. The mist clears and cruel laughter echoes in my head. Shit.

'Is it dead?'

I look around and see Punchy Des. He flinches as he sees me. 'Oh, man.' He turns and runs.

I feel empty. Not instantly. It's as if my soul is dissolving. I look at the rhino's horn. It's gone. I put a hand to my forehead. I feel an icy protrusion.

As the last of my humanity seeps away, I just have time to realise I didn't win. The rhino caught me.

I sniff the air and taste the aroma of Punchy Des, sweet with fear.

It's time to hunt.

~

ALTERNATIVE AFTERLIVES

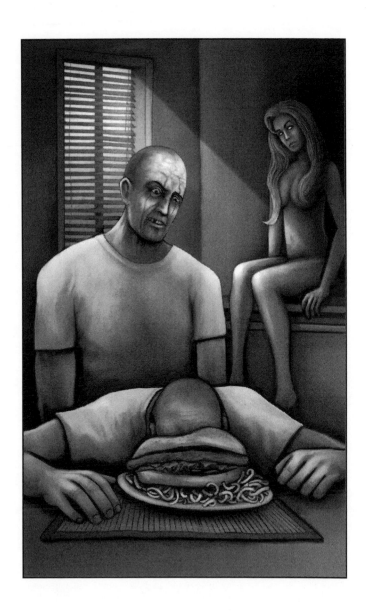

BLOODLESS

1

Mirrors don't lie. That's why I avoid them.

I know I ain't pretty. Got a broken nose. Teeth that make my tongue look like it's in prison. Face like a tattoo and scar crash.

I'm called Ton, because I weigh a ton. Well, I don't. Just look like I do. Me and the dark make nightmares together. But I'm 60. At 60, you can't contend. Not with men half your age, not with men a third your age. You're done.

I started out working in factories. Manual work. Lifting, moving, packing, boring. Wanted to do something different. Something better.

Joined a gym. Worked out. Boxed. Studied Krav Maga. Met people. Got invited to fight. Said, 'Yes.' The fight took place in a derelict warehouse. In a cage. No rules. I won. I wasn't just good, I was exceptional. I had speed, strength, stamina, power. No fear. No remorse. Gave me the advantage.

Worked hard. Became notorious. Gamblers loved me. King of the cage. Got a manager. He looked after me. Went legit. Earned good money. Kept on winning. I was unbeatable. Problem is, you're only unbeatable until Time takes you to bed and fucks you.

I had the sense to stop before I got beat. Actually, that ain't entirely true. My manager had the sense to make me stop before I got beat. My name became legend. Could Kane have taken me at my prime? Could Ruin? Maybe. We'll never know. They're now. I'm yesterday.

My manager thought I had a future hosting fights. Doing interviews. Running a gym. Shows how much he knew me. No reason to train meant no training. No training meant no routine. No routine meant no rules. No rules meant I could do whatever I wanted.

I had money. Not loads, but enough. For someone with sense. Problem is, sense ain't something I got a lot of. Spending's too easy. Women, booze, drugs. Moderation don't work for me. Didn't plan ahead. Got hooked on Blue Gold. Stupid name, seeing as it was white. Didn't matter what colour it was. Made me feel good. Snorted too much of it. Lost part of who I was. Ended up taking a bath in Shit Creek, using piss for shampoo.

Woke up one morning on the floor. In a bus stop. Covered in filth. My filth. It was lunchtime. People with jobs, with families, with lives, looking, staring, avoiding. Pity in their eyes. Disgust. Lowest I'd fallen. Not the lowest I'd fall.

I stumbled into an alley. Hid in a bin. Big metal dumpster. It stank. Rancid. But I felt better, away from people, out of sight.

Then a shadow gave me a little black card. Yeah, that's right. A shadow. Whoever it was, they looked like a shadow to me. Not sure how I got out the bin, or what I did in-between. I remember it was dark. I was in a kid's playground. Me and a few other fuckups, sleeping under a climbing frame. Felt the card being pressed into my hand. Opened my eyes. Saw the shadow. Gone before I could work out if I was dreaming. Thought it had given me money. Nearly threw the card away. Didn't. Noticed the design. Liked it. Gold writing, like sun rays. Title said: 'Witch Way?' Under that, it said: 'I deal in magic'. Then there was a phone number: '553700078'.

Things were bad. I wanted magic. Needed it. If the card wasn't a witch's, maybe it was a hooker's. Maybe she'd listen. Make me feel better. Used the last of my change to call. We talked. Turns out 'witch' wasn't a typo. She thought magic was real. Possible. I almost hung up. Almost.

Her voice was kind. Genuine. I listened to her. She was good with words. I decided to meet her. Find out if her witchcraft bullshit was witchcraft or bullshit.

She had a hut by the river. It looked like crap from the outside. Covered in weird graffiti. Made me think voodoo. Inside was different. Warm. Inviting. Safe.

She was remarkable. Striking. Angelic. Not like you'd imagine a witch to be. She wore a dress that hugged her curves. Multi-coloured. Looked like a paint factory had puked on it. She stared into my eyes and listened. Let me talk, tell her how shit things were. When I was done, she told me I was the one making things shit. I liked that about her. Her honesty.

Then she talked about magic. I was desperate. Wanted to believe her so bad. Told her I had no money. She didn't care. Told her I'd do anything. She gave me a contract. I signed it. Didn't read the bottom bit. You know, the bit written so small you can't read it. Wish I had.

She stuck a pin in my finger. Pulled her dress open. Smeared my blood on her chest, over her heart, and cast a spell.

I must have blacked out. Gone into a trance. Something... Not sure what happened, but when I came out of it, my head felt clear. Sober. I saw things from a distance. Saw my life how it really was. Saw me how I was.

I'd been a mess for a decade. Thought I was beyond salvation. Wished I was dead. Didn't have the courage to end it. Hoped the drugs or booze would do it for me.

Now I was considering the future. Being less of a prick. Someone I could be proud of. I was thinking about living life. Dreams. Aspirations. What I could be. Hadn't thought about that in years.

I smiled. It felt alien. Made me realise how long I'd been frowning. She had worked magic. Offered me hope. I was surprised to find I wanted it.

She watched me carefully. Made me tea. Watched me drink it. Gave me food. Watched me eat it. Made me promise to stay clean. I promised.

If I stayed clean, my life would be better. I'd be happy. I'd be alive. If I didn't, the magic would be wasted. I'd be back where I was, snorting, drinking, waking in bins, wishing I was dead. I promised again.

She took my hand, opened my fingers and pressed my palm onto her chest, over her heart. Her skin was soft. Warm. She looked into my eyes. Repeated herself. Insisted I live life, not endure it. I promised again. I don't know if she believed me. I think she wanted to.

2

I'd done good. For a while. Got a job. For a while. Went to the gym. For a while. Helped other wasters do better. For a while. Pictured the witch. For a while. Remembered her words. For a while. Lived clean. For a while. Fought the Cravings. For a while.

But then the clawing, niggling, itching, yearning... it hunted me. I tried to ignore it. Couldn't. Cravings always in my thoughts. In my dreams. Every moment of my existence consumed by want want want. Need need need. Relentless. Eternal. Maddening. Sometimes, the only way to stop the Cravings is to let them in. Accept there's no escape. Embrace them.

I stole. Bought drugs. Amphetamines. I like being wired. The energy. The power. Feeling immortal. Unstoppable. Like a storm. I got wasted.

I remember waking in mud and oil. Scrap metal place. Cars heaped around me. Moon in the sky. Silence. Complete silence. Puke and blood on my chest. My puke. My blood. A girl next to me. Naked. Wasted. A guy next to her. Bloody. More teeth on the floor next to him than in his mouth. Looked at my fists. Red. Bruised. Raw. Bite marks. Pain. It felt good. I smiled. Right then, I knew. Knew what I was. No amount of magic would help. No amount of trying. Pretending. I was no Samaritan. No priest. No good. No use. Nothing. I was an asshole. I was me.

Got up. Stared at the guy. His eyes moved to look at me. He groaned. Blood bubbled from his nose. Bone poked out of his arm. Caught the moonlight. Looked like a magic wand.

Went through his pockets. Found a wallet. Took the cash. Fuck him. Prick. Probably tried to rape the girl. Or me. There's usually a reason I get punchy. Unless I'm off my tits. Maybe he looked at me funny.

I was hungry. Lights in the distance. A town. Or the edge of a city. Dawn creeping through darkness. I walked towards the light. Looked for food.

3

I was eating a burger. Had some stupid name. Burger Me. Something like that. I'd spent the guy's cash on it. It was the size of a planet. Had its own centre of gravity. Curly fries were orbiting it. OK, I'm exaggerating. But it was big.

I'd only had one bite when I died. One. Then the burger went all see-through. Couldn't grip it. Dropped through my hands. I looked down and saw the back of my head, resting on the bun.

'Hello, Ton.' The voice was hypnotic. Laced with disappointment.

I looked up. The witch was sitting there, watching me. She was naked. Blonde hair fell over white skin, hiding her tits.

'My real name's Dennis,' I said. Needed her to know. Not sure why. Seemed important.

She shrugged. 'It doesn't matter. You broke your promise.' Her eyes were different. Unnatural. So bright they hurt. It was like looking at the sun. 'I expected more from you. Dennis.'

I looked at my knuckles. Still raw from the fight. Bloody and oozing.

I'd let her down. Let me down. Upset me so much it surprised me. My eyes felt like they might piss tears. I hid it. Coughed. Spat. Looked at her. Talked. I remember the conversation. Every word.

'Nice scythe,' I said. It was resting on the table. The blade was golden. Shone like the moon. 'I thought you were a witch.'

'I am.'

'Death is a witch?'

'I'm not Death. I'm Life.'

'You said your name was Meg.'

'You told me yours was Ton.'

Talking to her felt like I was losing a game. 'I'm dead, right?'

She nodded.

'So where's Death?'

'You gave me your soul.'

'When?'

'In the hut.'

'Did I fuck.'

'You should've read the small print. But it's a good thing. It means she can't have you.'

'She?'

'Death is my identical twin. Well, almost identical. Our eyes are different. On this side of mortality, mine are of stars. Hers are of the void. And she wears a cloak. I'm pure. Naked. Free. Alive.'

I looked down at the burger. I didn't feel hungry no more. 'What happens now?'

'You'll become Bloodless.'

'Bloodless?'

'Alive beyond death. Undead.'

'Like a zombie?'

'No. Nothing like that.'

'What then?'

'You'll be in my care. You'll spend eternity helping others. You'll guide mortals, help them understand what's important, what isn't, what they'll find fulfilling, how to find happiness. You'll tell them your story. You'll dispense magic.'

'What if I don't want to?'

'What you want is of no consequence.'

'Great. Your magic didn't work. Don't see why you should have me.'

'My magic worked perfectly. I gave you clarity. Sight. Perspective.'

'Didn't want clarity.'

'It's what you needed.'

'Still, didn't help, did it?'

'Yes, it did. It cleansed you. But you allowed your addiction to consume you. The magic worked. You failed.'

'And you still want me?'

'Yes. I see greatness in you, Dennis. By working with me, you might release that greatness and see it yourself.' She spoke softly. Every word filled with kindness. Hope. Belief in me. Me. An old prick who did so many drugs he's dead. My eyes were threatening to piss again.

'It's time.' She stood up. 'Embrace me.'

I got up. Did what she told me. Had to obey. She was beautiful. Perfect. But I felt no arousal. Just content in her arms. Protected. And protective. I don't know. I ain't good with words. Or feelings. Hard to explain it. I felt that maybe... maybe I wasn't all bad. I had something to give. And someone to guide me. A guardian. With her help, I could be someone of worth.

A wind began to swirl. Her embrace got tighter. Her lips pressed against mine. My mouth burned. I became hers. She was with me. In me. Everywhere.

She pulled away from me. Floated up. Her hair lashed about. Her eyes burned. She was power. She was beauty. She was everything. I was nothing. She looked down on me.

'You're of the ever now. You are unending. Of the sun and the stars. Of eternity. You're Bloodless.'

The wind scattered, exhausted. She floated down. Stood next to me. Took my hand. Led me out of the burger place. No one looked. No one cared. No one saw what I saw.

We stood on the street. The sun was bright but it didn't warm me. People didn't see me. Walked through me.

'You will be seen by those who seek something better,' said Life. 'Those who have the propensity to give everything in return for clarity. Those with hope. Those who seek magic.'

Then she taught me everything.

4

And now I'm sitting here, in Life's hut, talking to you.

She must see something in you. Hope. Strength. Something. Not everyone gets her number. Only those she can see inside. Only the few. You. You're special. Don't think you are. Think you ain't. But you don't know nothing. That's why you got a card from a shadow. Same one I did. You read the words. Couldn't ignore them. Couldn't forget them. Called the number.

I sat where you are. When I was desperate and living seemed pointless. I ain't perfect. Neither are you. I don't look like no witch. Neither do you. That don't mean we can't work magic. Do good. Just depends how we think. What we do. How we do it.

I can't tell you what happens if you face Death. I never done it, so I don't know. Even Life don't know. Says it ain't her business. Same way Death's got no business knowing what she does.

But Life says being Bloodless is a blessing. A gift. Makes you the best you can be. You know what? I'm starting to see it that way. OK, I admit, part of me wishes I'd read the small print. Chosen death. Faced Death. Been dead. I always wonder about it. Knowing I'll never know. Makes me restless. Like I missed a fight. A battle. Something better than I got. But that part of me – the asshole – is dying. I enjoy what I do. I learn all the time. I'm getting wiser. Slowly. Feeling complete. Whole. Somebody. I see that greatness Life told me about. I'm proud. Not of what I was. Or what I am. Of what I'm becoming.

I think Life's better at talking about this than me. She says that ain't true. I'm better. Sounds real coming from me, cos I've been where you are. Up Shit Creek, piss for shampoo and all that. Yeah. You know what I mean. Trying to escape. Nowhere to escape to. Wanting better. Not sure what better is. That's why you're here. Looking for magic.

I've said all I got to say. You know all you got to know. It's time for you to make a choice.

Here's a pen.

Here's a contract.

You gonna sign it?

~

A FINAL NOTE

Does anything await us beyond life?
We will all discover the answer to that question one day.
Let's just hope that day doesn't arrive too soon.

~

ACKNOWLEDGMENTS

Thank you to my editor, Edward Field.
www.squircle.me

Thank you to my proofreaders, Christie Cluett, David
Fielden, Edward Field, Georgie Fielden, John Gisby, Leah
Eades, Mark Fielden, Mark Rutterford, Mary Fielden,
Mel Ciavucco, Steph Minns and Tom Parker.

Thanks to David Whitlam for designing the book's cover
and creating the interior artwork.
www.davidwhitlam.com

Thanks to Marc Bessant for his technical assistance,
preparing the book for print.
www.marcbessant.com

Thanks to David Fielden for building and
maintaining my website.
www.bluetree.co.uk

Thank you to Consuelo Rivera-Fuentes, Jorge Vasquez,
Sophie Lloyd-Owen and everyone at Victorina Press for
having faith in my work and publishing this book.
www.victorinapress.com

~

APPENDIX

Short Story Publication History

Most of the stories in this book have been published before. You will find a full publication history below. Please note that the versions featured in this book have been edited extensively and some are very different to those previously published.

'Bloodless' was first published by *Writers' Forum*. It was later published by:
- Dark Lane Books, in *Dark Lane Anthology Volume 7*

'Death of a Superhero' was first published in the inaugural *To Hull And Back Short Story Anthology*. It was later published by:
- Arkbound, in *Boundless*
- Penny Shorts, as a digital download from their website
- Dark Lane Books, in *Dark Lane Anthology Volume 5*
- InkTears, in *Death of a Superhero*

'Devil's Crush' was first published in *Writers' Forum*. It was later published by:
- Chris Fielden, in *How to Write a Short Story, Get Published & Make Money* and the second *To Hull And Back Short Story Anthology*
- Dark Lane Books, in *Dark Lane Anthology Volume 5*
- InkTears, in *Death of a Superhero*

'Dirty Deeds, Done Dirt Cheap' was first published by Victorina Press, in this book.

'I Am The Warlock' was first published by Talent River. It was later published by:
- Chris Fielden, in *How to Write a Short Story, Get Published & Make Money*
- InkTears, in *Death of a Superhero*

'Mr Kill' was first published by The Brighton COW. It was later published by:
- Chris Fielden, in *How to Write a Short Story, Get Published & Make Money*
- *Katha Kshetre – Temple of Stories*
- Dark Lane Books, in *Dark Lane Anthology Volume 4*

'Shot In The Head And Left For Dead' was first published by World City Stories. It was later published by:
- Chris Fielden, in *How to Write a Short Story, Get Published & Make Money*

'The Cat, The Bull And The Madman' was first published by Laurel House Creative Workshops. It was later published by:
- Chris Fielden, in *How to Write a Short Story, Get Published & Make Money* and the third *To Hull And Back Short Story Anthology*

'The Day My Prayers Were Answered' was first published by *Writers' Forum*. It was later published by:
- Writing Short Fiction
- Chris Fielden, in *How to Write a Short Story, Get Published & Make Money*

'The El Paso Phantom Feeder' was first published by Darker Times in *Darker Times Anthology Volume 4*. It was later published by:

- Chris Fielden, in *How to Write a Short Story, Get Published & Make Money*

'The Keith of Death' was first published by *Writers' Forum*. It was later published by:

- InkTears, in *Death of a Superhero*
- Dark Lane Books, in *Dark Lane Anthology Volume 6*
- The Squat Pen Rests

'The Ninja Zombie Knitting Circle' was first published by Writers' Village. It was later published by:

- Chris Fielden, in *How to Write a Short Story, Get Published & Make Money* and the fourth *To Hull And Back Short Story Anthology*

'The Treasure No Thief Can Steal' was first published by Park Publications in *Scribble*. It was later published by:

- Chris Fielden, in *How to Write a Short Story, Get Published & Make Money*

'Troll's Head' was first published by Chris Fielden, in *How to Write a Short Story, Get Published & Make Money*. It was later published by:

- InkTears, in *Death of a Superhero*

~

Chris was born in in the 1970s, which is too long ago for his liking. He grew up in Portishead, a town in the South West of England, and has lived in the Bristol area for most of his life.

He has played drums in rock bands for over 30 years and has been fortunate enough to tour all over the world.

Chris self-published his first novel, *Wicked Game*, in 2010. To avoid a mental breakdown, he then started writing short stories as they're a lot easier to finish.

Since then, Chris has become an award-winning and Amazon bestselling author. He's been published extensively by independent press, established magazines and renowned websites.

Book of the Bloodless Volume 2 is a work in progress and Chris hopes to finish it before he has to don his own superhero costume and face the reaper.

You can find out more about Chris on his website: www.christopherfielden.com

Photo by Thomas David Parker